DISCOVERED SUSPICION

DISCOVERED SUSPICION

JULIE BAWDEN DAVIS

Roses
A R E
RED
PUBLISHING

ACKNOWLEDGMENTS

As they say, it takes a village. Here's my village. I'm supremely grateful to each of these fabulous people!

ARC Reading Gems
Julie Schlueter
Tara Bradley
Susa Fraccaroli
Kery Bailey
Trish Darrenkamp
Marilyn Smith
Lisa Starkey
Beth Helm
Teresa Reitnauer
Chelle Young
Asra Syed
Jacquelyn Gray
Penny McCulloch
Ellen White
Karen McTyeire
Heather Wamboldt
Amber Mancebo

Pros
Sharon Whatley, editing
Judy Bullard, cover design
Kyle Kane, logo design
Sabrina Wildermuth, design consultation
Jeremy Davis, technical support

To those who have lost loved ones.

PROLOGUE

March 18, 1995, Camp Pendleton, Oceanside, California

"Blow out the candles. You're so slow."

"Patrick, your sister is only six. Let her be," said their mother, who jiggled their baby brother, Tad, on one hip as she took a quart of strawberry ice cream out of the freezer.

"Let me help you, then we can eat the cake." Patrick's tone was less harsh now. "I'll count, then we both blow, okay?"

Cherie, frilly white dress, pink bows in her hair, looked up at her big brother, who gave her an encouraging smile.

"Get ready, Cherie. Five, four, three, two, one."

The brother and sister leaned together and blew, extinguishing the candles. Cherie clapped with excitement.

"Can I cut the cake, Mom?" said Patrick.

Their mother pulled a cake knife out of a drawer and handed it to him. Just then the doorbell rang. "I know you're ten going on forty, Patrick, but be careful with the knife," she said, walking out of the room to get the door.

"How big of a piece do you want?" Patrick held the knife over the cake, decorated in pink icing and blue sprinkles.

Cherie took advantage of her mother's absence and said in a loud whisper, "Really big."

Patrick slid a giant slice onto her plate as their mother cried out from the front room. "You stay here," Patrick said, setting down the knife.

Cherie began eating the sprinkles off her birthday cake, jumping when she heard her brother yell. She hurried out of the kitchen and saw her mother sitting on the floor, her back up against the couch. Through the living room's bay window, Cherie could see a man in uniform walking down their front steps.

"What's wrong, Mama?" Cherie asked.

Patrick held the baby tight to his chest. His eyes looked scared. "It's Dad."

"What's wrong with Daddy?" asked Cherie.

"He's not coming home," said Patrick.

"Why not?" She started to cry as her mother put her head in her hands and began sobbing.

"He went to heaven," said Patrick, then walked out of the room.

1

Present Day, Dulles International Airport

Cherie Tomlinson set her carry-on next to her at the airport café. Finally, the vacation she'd been dreaming about for months. She smiled when the waitress approached, setting a glass of water in front of her.

"What can I get you, honey?"

Cherie decided to celebrate. "A Mai Tai," she said, then added, "with extra lime."

"You got it," said the waitress, turning to take the next table's order.

Cherie looked over to see an especially handsome man dressed in khakis, a dark-blue turtleneck, and loafers. He had close-cropped black hair and wore the sexy stubble of someone who hadn't shaved for a couple of days. When he finished ordering, he glanced at Cherie. She wanted to look away but didn't want to appear rude.

"Are you coming or going?" the man asked.

"Me?"

He laughed. "Yes."

Cherie pulled a napkin from the dispenser on the table and replied, "Going. Puerto Vallarta." She dabbed at several drips of water from the glass on the front of her green sweater and tan slacks.

"It just so happens that I'm also going to Puerto Vallarta," he said as the waitress put Cherie's Mai Tai in front of her, then handed the mystery man a beer. "May I?" he asked, gesturing with his head at the other seat at her table.

Cherie nodded awkwardly, then managed to reply, "Of course."

The man stood and came toward her. He was muscular, his biceps and pecs apparent through his shirt. He sat down and asked, "Are you from the DC area?"

"I am," she said, taking a drink of the Mai Tai, hoping the alcohol would ease a sudden feeling of shyness that had cropped up. "Are you from here?"

He took a sip of his beer and replied, "Just passing through." He stuck out his hand. "I'm Justin."

Cherie took his hand, warm and firm, and they shook. "Cherie."

"So, what kind of work do you do?" he asked her.

"I work in a government job." Her boss had emphasized more than once it was best not to let people know she was FBI.

"Sounds mysterious," he said, smiling.

"What about you?"

"I'm a painter."

"Oh, as in artist?" asked Cherie.

He laughed. "No, buildings and such."

Just then, a voice came over the intercom, announcing it was time to board their flight. Cherie reached for her bag.

Justin stood, fishing a twenty from his pocket to lay on the table. "I've got your drink. After you."

"That wasn't necessary, but thank you," she said.

As they exited the café and headed across the corridor for their gate, a military policeman walked by, the letters MP emblazoned on his shirt. Cherie stopped as he passed, curious as to what could be going on. Then before she knew what was happening, Justin clasped his arm around her waist and pulled her close. Startled, she looked up to see he had pulled a baseball cap low over his face.

"Keep walking slowly to the gate," he said in a low voice.

Cherie wanted to cry out but was afraid he might have a weapon. All she could think of was to get as far away from this man as possible, but he held her tight.

"What do you want?" she said, grimacing as she tried to pull free.

"Please, just go along with this, and I'll explain it all once we're in the air."

"Are you armed?" Cherie asked as they approached an agent checking tickets.

"No, of course not." He kept pressure on her waist, his body close to hers.

Again, she thought of yelling out but didn't want to find out he had a gun after all.

The agent reached out her hand and said, "Passports and tickets, please."

Cherie handed hers over, and the agent scanned and returned her documents. Then Justin gave her his. Cherie held her breath as the woman checked his and handed them back, calling to the passenger behind them, "Next."

Justin nudged her forward onto the loading ramp toward the plane as a high-pitched whine filled the air from the jet's engines. Once they had boarded, he let go of Cherie and said in a quiet tone, "Thank you for going along with that."

When they got to a set of seats where a woman sat, Justin stopped and said, "I'm here."

Cherie kept walking, soon locating her seat. She sat down next to the window and placed her bag on the floor in front of her. Clasping her hands, she noted that her heart still raced in her chest. What if she rang for the flight attendant and told him she was FBI and asked to speak to the US Marshal onboard? But what would she say? That a man had insisted on boarding with her? She looked out at the tarmac dotted with day's-old, dirty snow and steadied her breathing. As they waited for the plane to take off, she half expected the MPs to board and pull Justin off. But before long the flight attendant came on the intercom, his voice bright. "Welcome aboard flight 5587 to Puerto Vallarta. We'll be in the air for seven hours and twenty-five minutes. The captain has put on the fasten your seatbelt sign."

Justin Kincaid breathed a sigh of relief when they were officially out of US airspace. They'd been flying for a few hours when he decided to stretch his legs. He walked partway down the aisle to see the woman who he'd boarded the plane with asleep in her seat. With her face peaceful, she was even more pretty. Her dark lashes lay against her cheeks, her brown hair sleek and silky on her shoulders. He owed her an explanation and had meant it when he said he would untangle his strange behavior once they were on the plane. But feeling certain he would never encounter the woman again, decided against it. What would be the point? He had boarded, and for the moment was safe.

The memory of the last twenty-four hours thrumming in his head, he turned and walked back down the aisle, checking his watch as he did so. It was 1100 hours. He'd be in Mexico at 0200 hours. Hopefully, they hadn't yet figured out he'd left the country.

2

Cherie hung back until Justin disembarked. Afraid of what he might do next, she wanted as much distance as possible between the two of them.

When she walked out into the balmy night and headed toward the baggage claim, she welcomed the rush of warm air across her skin. It had been a cold winter back in DC. As she approached the luggage circling the carousel, Cherie glanced around. No sign of Justin. She pulled up the rideshare app on her phone and ordered a car. While waiting for her bag, she replayed the bizarre encounter with Justin in her head, but still couldn't make sense of it. As her mind continued to whir, she saw her bag pop out of the chute at the top of the carousel and thump down. She looped her way past a couple waiting, hoisted it off, then headed outside to wait for her ride.

Justin called his buddy, Billy, who lived in the mountains of Puerto Vallarta, but there was no answer. He stood in the shadows outside of the airport, nearly deserted at this late hour, assessing his best next move. Just then Cherie came out, her phone in hand. The woman intrigued him. She came across as very cautious, glancing around constantly, hyper-aware of her surroundings.

A few minutes later when an older, gray Honda pulled up, she moved tentatively toward the car and checked her phone and the license plate. The driver got out and came toward her, but she backed up.

"*Está bien*," said the man. "It's okay, lady."

"Where's your Uber decal?" she asked. "I want to see identification before I get into your car."

"Get in the car. I will show you."

"I'm not going anywhere with you," said Cherie loudly. She moved toward the building, pulling her suitcase with her.

He shouted then, "Regalio!"

The rear door of the car opened then, and another man jumped out brandishing a knife in one hand. He rushed toward Cherie. Justin sprang out of the shadows toward the man with the knife and tackled him, swiftly wrestling the gleaming steel blade from his grasp and sending the man flying across the pavement. As he did so, the driver grabbed Justin around the neck from behind. Justin elbowed him hard in the gut, breaking his grasp, then spun around and sliced the driver's arm.

"*Pendejo*," the driver cussed, grasping his arm as the blood came quickly. The other man charged at Justin then, but Justin sucker punched him in the face, knocking him to the pavement again. Then he pointed to the Honda, still idling, and said to Cherie, "Get in!"

She looked uncertain for a moment, then ran to the car

and jumped in the passenger seat as Justin got in the driver's seat and floored it. In the rearview mirror, he could see one of the guys running after them.

As he raced away from the airport, he glanced over at her. "You okay?"

"I'm fine," she said, her eyes round. "I should be asking if you're okay."

Justin looked in the back, noting a car seat. "My guess is this car is stolen."

"Where are you going?" she asked him.

"A buddy has a place in the mountains outside of the city. I'm waiting to hear from him, but in the meantime, we'll head that way."

"I have a hotel that I already paid for. You can drop me off there. It's the Sands Resort."

"In case you hadn't noticed, those guys were after you," said Justin, looking at her, then back at the road. "Most likely for ransom. If they wanted to rob you, they would have taken your bag."

"Ransom?" The fine line of her brows knitted with concern. "Drop me at my hotel. I'll be fine."

"And what are you going to do when you run into one of those guys in town?"

"How do I know that you aren't kidnapping me for ransom?" said Cherie. "This could be one big ploy to get me alone."

"Believe me. The last thing I had planned on was rescuing you and stealing a car. I've got a lot bigger problems. To prove to you that I mean you no harm, I'll drop you off at your hotel. It's on the way to the mountains."

Still shaken from what had just occurred, Cherie tried to unscramble her brain. While she had heard things could be dangerous in Mexico, she didn't think she'd be attacked as soon as she arrived. If she did run into those men again, she was no match for them—especially without her gun. She had considered registering it and bringing it with her but didn't think she'd need it.

"How far until the hotel?"

"I'd say another fifteen minutes."

"Where'd you learn to fight like that?" she asked, keeping her tone casual.

He gave her a sidelong glance. "Here and there."

His phone rang then, and he pulled it out and answered. "Hey, yeah. It's a burner. Where are you?" She watched his forehead crease in question. "Alright, I was hoping you'd be here. I—." He glanced at Cherie. "Let's just say, things are unraveling. I think I remember the way." As he put his phone down and took the wheel with both hands, Cherie noticed blood pooling on his forearm.

"You're hurt," she said.

He glanced at his arm. "I've been much worse."

A few minutes later, Cherie saw her hotel in the distance.

"You can just drop me off at the gate."

"I'm driving all the way up and making sure you get in safely," he said matter-of-factly.

As they approached the resort, Cherie wondered if it was true that she had been targeted at the airport. The thought of encountering the men again made her insides shiver.

3

"I changed my mind," said Cherie.

Justin snapped his head around and looked at her. "What?"

"You're right. I might not be safe at the hotel. Keep driving."

He continued for a short distance, then pulled the car over to the side of the road, yards from the entrance to the hotel. Turning to face her, he said, "To be honest, you might be in more danger with me." He glanced out the windshield, then back at her.

Cherie looked into Justin's eyes, something telling her that he wasn't a bad guy. She took a deep breath and asked, "What or who are you running from?"

He ran his hand over the stubble on his face and replied, "The less you know, the safer you are."

Everything in Cherie wanted to tell him she was FBI, and that maybe she and her team could help. But if he was a fugitive, her only recourse would be to take him in.

"You seem like a really nice woman," he said. "I don't think you want to get mixed up in this."

Cherie glanced at the hotel, lit up against the dark sky. "How about you take me wherever you're going. In the morning, I'll figure a way out that doesn't involve you. Will that work?" she asked him.

Car lights flashed in the rearview mirror. They both turned their heads.

"That car is coming pretty fast," she said.

Justin gunned the engine and hurtled back onto the highway. When they were some distance away, Cherie commented, "They turned into the hotel."

"Three am seems a little late to check in," he said.

Cherie shifted in her seat, the realization of being followed disturbing.

"You said you work for the government. What branch?" asked Justin. He kept his eyes straight ahead.

Cherie blurted out, "The post office."

"You're a mail carrier?"

"No, I work in the main office in administration." She held her breath, waiting to see his reaction. When she saw his shoulders relax out of the corner of her eye, she quietly exhaled.

Justin turned on the radio and welcomed the sound of salsa as it filled the car. It was like this since he got back from the last assignment. Sometimes he just needed to drown out the cacophony in his mind. After a bit, he stole a glance at Cherie, who appeared to be resting, eyes closed. When she told him she worked for the post office, she seemed legit. But something was niggling him about her. He just couldn't figure out what.

Before long, the road began to incline, and they were soon crawling up the mountain. If he recalled correctly, the turnoff was just up ahead. He glanced at the gas gauge. None too soon, either. They'd be running on fumes before long.

Cherie observed Justin through lowered lids as he drummed his fingers on the steering wheel. She was supposed to be spending her first night in Mexico in a luxury suite, but instead she was on her way to where? A house in the woods? With a stranger? She ran through what had occurred over the last couple of hours and came to the same conclusion. She was better off with Justin. Her instincts screamed that the car heading into the hotel carried the men who had been after her at the airport. And Cherie had learned from an early age the importance of paying attention to her instincts.

"C'mon Cherie. I know they're older guys, but they're cool." She was at her friend Kayla's house, and her parents weren't home.

"This seems like a bad idea," said Cherie, feeling increasingly uneasy. "How many guys are coming?" She watched as her friend ran a tube of bright pink lipstick across her mouth.

"Three or four of them," said Kayla. "They're bringing some beer, too."

"Beer?" said Cherie, the alarm bells now ringing so loudly in her ears she felt short of breath. "Call them back and tell them not to come."

Kayla pushed her long blonde hair over her shoulders and huffed. "And say what? My friend Cherie is chicken?"

"Remind them we're only in eighth grade!"

"One of the guys is on the football team. He's really cute."

Seeing that she wasn't going to change her friend's mind, Cherie got up and left the room.

"Where are you going?" Kayla called after her.

"To the bathroom," said Cherie. She went into Kayla's parents' room and picked up the phone, punching in her home number.

"Patrick, it's me."

"What's up?"

"Kayla invited a bunch of older guys over, and her parents aren't home. I think something bad might happen."

"I'll be right over."

When the doorbell rang a few minutes later and Kayla flounced to open it, Cherie was relieved to see her brother standing there, his lanky frame backlit by the porchlight.

"What are you doing here?" asked Kayla, irritation in her tone. She looked from him to Cherie.

When her brother didn't reply, Cherie spoke up. "I called him. I don't think it's a good idea to have boys over here when your parents aren't home, Kayla."

Her friend swung around, hands on hips. "You are such a goody two-shoes!"

Just then, a car pulled up in the driveway, and several

doors opened and slammed shut. Four guys came walking up the front path, the one in the lead crying out, "What the hell are you doing here, Tomlinson?"

When the car stopped a few minutes later, Justin shut off the engine, keeping the headlights on. Cherie sat up to see the front of a small house. It was hard to make out anything else in the dark night.

"This is your friend's place?" she asked.

"Yeah, he's fishing off the coast of Mazatlán, but he told me where the spare key is. You can stay in the car while I go and get it."

"Before you go," said Cherie.

Justin looked at her in the dim light and waited.

"Thank you for coming to my rescue at the airport. You didn't have to, but you did, and I appreciate it."

"You're wrong about one thing," Justin said, his face serious. "I did have to."

4

Cherie watched Justin disappear around the side of the house. A few minutes later, he pulled open the driver's side door and leaned in. "I couldn't find the key. He's pretty forgetful." He thought for a minute. "I hate to break a window."

"I can get the door open," said Cherie. She unzipped her purse and took out a credit card.

Justin looked at her, surprise in his eyes. "You pick locks?"

"My older brother taught me." She got out of the car and headed toward the front door, asking over her shoulder, "Does your friend have an alarm system?"

"No. You need some light?" Justin came to stand behind her.

"I can do it by feel." Cherie slid the card into the space between the door and the jamb and shimmied it up and down. Nothing. She removed it, flipped it over, continuing to work it along the crack until, at last, the lock gave. Then she turned the knob and opened the door.

"Let me make sure all is clear," said Justin.

Cherie stepped aside so he could enter.

Justin turned on the light, revealing a crowded space. Books and newspapers were stacked on tabletops, along with a week's worth of dirty coffee cups. What looked like half of his friend's wardrobe lay scattered across the floor.

"I take it he's also disorganized," said Cherie from the doorstep.

Justin took everything in, then went down a short hallway. She heard him open a couple of doors before returning. "You can come in. Just make sure the door is locked. Dead bolt, if there is one."

Cherie walked in, noting the fatigue in Justin's body as he moved about the house. Even not looking his best, he was still incredibly handsome. She glanced around the room. Next to a ratty sofa sat a coffee table littered with dirty dishes. Across the room in a small kitchen the faucet dripped into a skillet in the sink.

"At least we're safe for now." She wheeled her suitcase next to the couch and looked down at a disarray of throw pillows. "I'll get some shut-eye, then figure out things in the morning and get out of your hair," she said.

"You can have the bed. It's in the back. I insist," he said.

"Okay," said Cherie, hoping the bed would be decent, then headed down the hallway. When she turned to say goodnight to Justin, he walked up right behind her. She jumped and stopped.

"I'm sorry," he said. "I was just going to say that before you go into the room, I'd like to get some clean clothes."

Justin sorted through Billy's clothing, looking for some-

thing that would fit. As he continued to search, he wondered
about how she effortlessly picked the lock. "So, are you and
your brother close?" He pushed a drawer closed and turned
to face her.

Cherie's face clouded over. "We were, yes."

"Sounds like there's a story there."

"We're still close, but..." She left her sentence unfinished.

"Forget it. It's not my business. I'll let you get some rest."
He turned to leave. "Would you like to get into the bathroom
first, freshen up?"

"It's fine. Go ahead," she said, leaning down to unzip her
suitcase.

After a quick shower and change of clothes, Justin went
out into the living room, where he checked the lock on the
door. He turned off the light, plunging the room into darkness, then went to the couch and stretched out, putting his
arms under his head. Hopefully he could get at least a few
hours of sleep, so he could think straight and figure out his
next moves. He was quickly running out of time.

It was still night when Cherie startled awake to the sound
of Justin's voice. She swung her legs to the edge of the bed
and sat there, heart banging in her chest. Afraid something
was wrong, she strained to listen. It sounded like he was
talking to someone. Unless Billy had returned, who would be
here at this hour? She slid out of bed and yanked off her
nightgown, quickly pulling on a skirt and shirt, then padded
barefoot to the door, putting her ear to it. Unable to catch
the words, she flipped on the light in the room and glanced

around for a weapon, seeing a bat in the corner. She grabbed it and switched the light back off, then quietly turned the bedroom doorknob and stepped out into the hallway. Engulfed in darkness, she felt her way along the wall to the living room.

"Yes, sir. Understood," Justin mumbled. "Conceal and contain the enemy."

Cherie's fear level spiked. Was he referring to her? She pressed herself against the hallway wall and listened. Several seconds passed, then Justin shouted, "Credible threat!"

Pushing away from the wall, she crept into the living room, her eyes adjusting to the dim light. As she walked softly to where he lay, she tried not to make a sound. When she stood beside him, she looked down to see he still slept. There was no one else in the room. He began tossing and turning then, and a pained mix of emotions crossed his face. She was about to retreat to her room when he opened his eyes. He reached up and grabbed her by the arm, startling her. She let out a cry and tried to pull away.

"What do you want?" he demanded.

His grip was like a vice, hurting her, and she called out his name.

Recognition flooded his eyes then, and he let go of her arm.

"I heard voices. I just wanted to make sure everything was okay," she said.

He saw the bat in her hand and sat up. "Is something happening?"

Cherie dropped the bat to the floor, her heart still hammering in her ears. "I thought someone had broken in." She stood there as he stared at her. "You're military?" she asked, finally. She had no other choice but to be blunt.

His eyes narrowed slightly.

"You were yelling about enemies and credible threats," she said.

His expression relaxed. "I'm sorry. I didn't mean to wake you." He rubbed both hands over his face.

Cherie went to the window, noting that the sky was beginning to lighten. "My father was military," she murmured.

"Was?"

"Afghanistan. He died in combat when I was young," said Cherie, surprising herself for revealing something few people knew.

"I'm sorry to hear that," said Justin. His tone sounded sincere.

Cherie took several steps toward him. "You need to be straight with me," she said simply. "I want to know who you are and what's going on, before we both get killed."

Justin glanced out the window. "It looks like it will be morning soon," he said, avoiding her question. "Let me see if Billy has some coffee." He got up and went into the kitchen and began opening cupboards.

Cherie followed, a mixture of anxiety and anger bubbling up inside her. Yanking the refrigerator door open, she located a bag of grounds and shoved it against his chest.

"Did you want a cup?" he asked, taking the bag without looking at her.

"Yes."

He located the coffee machine and got it started, then turned to lean against the counter, crossing his arms over his chest. As the water in the machine began percolating, Justin said, "To answer your question, yes, I'm military."

Cherie thought of the MP at the airport and had a sudden thought. "Are you AWOL?"

Justin abruptly pushed away from the counter. "Who are you, really?"

5

Cherie stared directly into Justin's eyes, waiting for his answer. They remained that way for a long moment, then she broke the silence. "You said you had to save me from those men at the airport. Why?"

Justin started to answer, then backed up slightly, studying her. He took his time. "You didn't answer my question. Who are you?"

"You didn't answer either of my questions." Cherie stood up straighter and folded her arms across her chest. She waited, unsure if she wanted to hear his answer.

There was something about the easy way this woman held herself that Justin admired. How rather than back down, she suddenly produced what looked like a steel backbone.

"I bet a lot of people underestimate you," he said after some silence.

Surprise momentarily crossed her face. "Why do you say that?"

"That's another question, and you haven't answered mine."

"It appears we're at a standstill," said Cherie, her expression unmoving now.

"It's best for your safety that I don't tell you anything more than you may have already conjectured," said Justin.

Cherie started to reply when there was movement outside the front door. Justin picked the bat off the floor and approached the door, ready to swing. A key sounded in the lock and the knob turned. Billy stood on the threshold.

The guy wore cutoff jean shorts and a tank top, a red bandana on his head. He set a fishing pole up against the wall next to the door. "Whoa, bro," he said, then looked at Cherie. "Who's she?"

"We were just discussing that," said Justin, setting the bat down beside the couch. "Some guys tried to grab her last night at the airport. I stepped in, and here we are."

The man shook his head. He seemed to size up the situation he'd walked into, then glanced toward the kitchen. "Is that coffee I smell?" He walked across the room and poured himself a mug, then opened a cupboard and pulled out a bottle of whiskey, adding a few splashes. After taking a long, careful sip, he said, "Ahh, that's exactly what I needed." Then he leaned against the cluttered kitchen counter. "About those men that tried to nab you, Miss?"

"Cherie. You're Billy?"

"Yeah, and this is my palace," he said, gesturing around him. "There's been a bunch of tourist kidnappings lately. You're lucky Justin was there."

"What happens to the victims? Is it for ransom?"

"Sorry, but I gotta get a load off. I pulled my back out yesterday." Billy went to the living room area and sat down on the couch. He took another sip of the steaming coffee, then replied, "As far as I've heard, they're disappearing. That's what's so wild about it. No one's been able to track a single person down."

Cherie hadn't heard anything about this when she checked out the area before booking her flight here. Was this guy just a blowhard? Did he even know what he was talking about?

"How long has this been going on?" she asked.

"Awhile now, from what I hear, but it's gotten worse lately." He pushed some books and yellowed newspapers out of the way and set the mug on the end table next to the couch. "If you're here for a vacation, you might want to consider going back home. It's not worth disappearing to who knows where."

Cherie thought for a moment. If she booked a flight right now, she could be home, or better yet, another safer destination, maybe even by tonight.

"Excuse me," she said and grabbed her purse.

"If you stand at the back of the house, the reception is pretty good," said Billy.

Cherie could feel their eyes on her as she left, then they began talking. She stood there for a moment outside the door, straining to see if she could make anything out, but all she heard was the murmur of voices.

"Patrick, where were you?" Cherie bolted up from the couch. She'd been waiting there for hours after hearing her brother sneak out of the house.

"What are you doing up, Sis? You have school tomorrow."

"So do you," said Cherie, fourteen at the time. "Where did you go?" She noted for the first time that he had his backpack, and it appeared full.

"I was out," he said, gingerly setting the pack down in the hallway.

"What's in there?" she asked, worried there was something that could get him in trouble.

"Just some gym clothes. I haven't cleaned it out in a while. You need to go to bed before Mom gets home."

"She's working until morning, like always."

"Whatever. Go to bed."

Cherie glanced at the backpack again. "I don't like it when you leave me and Tad alone at night. You're supposed to be here."

"I won't do it again, okay? Now go get some sleep."

Cherie turned and headed toward her bedroom. As she settled back down in bed, she decided. In the morning, she was going to see what was in that backpack.

Cherie dialed the airline and repeated "agent" into the phone multiple times, until a real person finally came on the line.

"How can I assist you today?"

"Something has come up. I need to leave Puerto Vallarta as soon as possible." She gave the woman her flight information.

"Back to Dulles, ma'am?"

Cherie looked out at the surrounding jungle terrain as she spoke, the lush green vegetation lightening as the day dawned. "Do you have any flights to Hawaii?"

"Which island, ma'am?"

"Any of them."

"One moment, please."

After a bit, the agent said, "The next available flight to Honolulu is tomorrow afternoon. Leaving from Mexico City."

Cherie recalled the map of Mexico she had studied. The capital was hours away.

"What about the Bahamas?"

After a few frustrating attempts to find a destination that wouldn't require traveling to Mexico City or waiting several days to leave, Cherie finally said, "Just get me a flight back to Dulles from Puerto Vallarta, please." She would go home, regroup, and then get another flight out.

As she waited for the agent to finish the transaction, she noticed the sun edging up off the horizon, casting a lovely golden glow. The shrubbery rustled and a pheasant walked out. She stood still watching as it poked around in the dirt. When the bird saw her, it scuttled off.

This was the kind of environment she'd been looking for when she booked this vacation. Something out of the ordinary. Was she overreacting changing her flight? She was taking the word of a man who put whiskey in his morning coffee.

6

When she went back in the house, the talking stopped and both men turned to her.

"I've got a flight out tomorrow." She addressed Billy. "Maybe you could drive me to my hotel? I can get a ride from there to the airport in the morning."

Billy looked at Justin.

"I can pay you," said Cherie.

"I'm pretty beat," said Billy, yawning.

Exasperation surged through Cherie, but she kept her voice even. "Can I call for someone to come pick me up then?"

"No!" said both men in unison.

She turned to Justin. "I asked Billy because it seems you're trying to lie low, but could you drop me at the hotel?"

Justin hesitated. "What if those men go back to find you?"

"It's only for a night. I'll just stay in my room."

A few minutes later, they headed away from Billy's house. Justin snuck glances at Cherie out of the corner of his eye. He still wanted to know her real story, but there was no point now. He turned on Billy's radio to a scratchy AM station as salsa tunes filled the car.

When they neared the hotel, a black sedan approached from the other direction. Justin glanced at the driver as they sped past. Was that Warner? A high-pitched warning sounded in his ears as he slowed and neared the hotel driveway.

"You can just drop me off."

"I think it's better if I make sure you get into your room safely." They drove down a long driveway past palms towering into the blue sky until they came to the roundabout in front of the lobby doors.

Justin pulled out his burner phone. "Just give me one minute to make a call," he said, then dialed Billy's number, praying his friend would pick up. Finally, after the call nearly went to voicemail, Billy answered. "Just a second," he said to Cherie, hopping out of the car and walking a few paces away as he spoke. "Billy, you there?"

"Justin, you woke me up, man."

"I'm pretty sure I saw Warner on his way to your place."

"Shit."

"I've got your car. The other one is hot, but it works. Keys are in the ignition."

"Fuck."

"What?"

"He's here."

"I'll be there as soon as I can," said Justin.

"Don't come. I'm not telling them I saw you."

Justin hung up the call and opened the passenger door, willing himself to take even breaths. He gestured to the lobby doors. "Let's get you checked in."

Cherie gave him an odd look. "Are you okay?"

"I'm fine." He waited for her to get out of the car, then shut and locked it. In the lobby, a young woman greeted them in Spanish. "*Buenos días*. Are you both checking in?"

"Actually, the reservation is mine. Cherie Tomlinson. I was supposed to check in last night, but I got held up."

"Good news. We still have your room available," said the clerk, typing quickly on her keyboard. "It's on the second floor overlooking the pool." She took out two keycards and handed them to Cherie.

Justin was hiding it well, but Cherie could tell he was nervous. Sweat beaded his brow, and his hand trembled slightly when he took her suitcase from her.

When they arrived at her room, he announced, "Well, here you are." He set her suitcase next to the door.

"Here I am," said Cherie. "Thank you for getting me to my room, and again for helping me last night. I hope you get everything worked out."

"I'm sure I will," said Justin. "Just a few things to sort through."

Cherie held his gaze for an awkward moment, then she slid the keycard in, and the light turned green. When she pushed open the door, he said, "Safe travels back to the States." Then he started down the hallway.

"Wait!" Cherie heard herself saying.

Justin turned around.

"Did you want to come in for..." she faltered. She didn't even know why she was saying this. "....a drink of water?"

Justin's brow relaxed slightly. "Sure," he said.

Inside, she set her things down in the entryway.

"Nice place," said Justin, glancing around the room and nodding in approval.

Cherie had splurged on the room, pleased with its compact but stylish sitting area and cozy bed adorned with a blue and green bedspread. A stainless steel and glass coffee table sat in front of a small, red couch, on it a vase filled with tropical flowers. The carpet felt plush under her feet as she walked over to a minifridge and pulled it open, then handed Justin a water bottle. He removed the lid and drank half of it down in several gulps.

"The sedan that passed. Was that someone you know?" Cherie asked after opening her bottle and taking several sips. "It seemed to rattle you."

Justin perched on the edge of the couch, looking defeated. Then he put his head in his hands.

Cherie knew she should stay out of this, but something about the way he looked at that moment—so alone—spoke to her, and she couldn't help herself. "What are you running from, Justin? I've spent enough time with you to know you're not a bad person. Instead of making things worse, why not just turn yourself in?"

Justin shook his head. "You don't understand. I can't do that."

"If you tell me, I will understand, and I might be able to help you."

Justin stood and began pacing. "No one can help me, but me. If there's anything I've learned over the last few months, that is at the top of the list."

"Try me," said Cherie. "I'm good at problem solving."

Justin stopped and looked at her. "This problem is much bigger than you and I and even Billy put together. I appreciate you wanting to help, but there are certain things I have to take care of myself."

Cherie knew she should get on the plane tomorrow and forget this ever happened. But she didn't think she could do that. She faced him. "Tell me what you're running from, and I'll tell you where I really work."

Justin considered her words for a moment. Then he looked directly into her eyes. "I've been framed by the US military. I can't go back to the States until I clear my name. If I go back now, they are going to court martial me."

Cherie studied Justin's face. When someone was lying, they tended to not meet your eyes, or there was a tell, like a twitch. Justin showed neither. More importantly, her gut told her he was telling the truth.

"Okay, you asked who I really am." She hesitated, not wanting her words to create a feeling of mistrust. "I'm an FBI agent."

7

Justin backed up as if Cherie had just told him she was an assassin.

"I meant it when I said I want to help," she said.

He gave her a dubious look, so she continued. "I still owe you for saving me. Let me help save you." Cherie headed to the couch and sat down.

For a time, Justin just stood there. He tensed when there was movement outside the door, then voices as a group of people walked down the hall. She leaned back against the couch cushions. Now that she was sitting down, the adrenaline started to ebb.

"What office do you work at?" Justin asked.

"DC."

"So Bureau headquarters."

"Yes."

"How long?"

"It's your turn to answer a question." She looked up at him. "Please just sit down."

Justin grabbed a chair from against the wall and brought it over. He turned it around to face her, then straddled it.

Cherie reached for her water bottle on the coffee table. "You've told me you're military, and you're obviously trained in combat. But if you're being framed, that couldn't be your only specialty."

Justin didn't know what to make of this woman. First, she works for the post office, now she's an FBI agent. He thought about how he'd been keeping this all bottled up, though, and she was so easy to talk to. "Cryptology is my main specialty."

"So, you're a cyber expert. And Billy? How does he fit into all of this?"

"He and I served together. He got out at ten years. I opted to stay. Which I realize now was a bad idea. Look, you're a nice person. I don't want to get you involved in all of this. It's best I just go." He stood up.

"Where are you going to go?"

Justin held the back of the chair, tightening his grip. He was so tired of feeling boxed in.

"To check on Billy."

Cherie sat up. "Look, it's too late to not involve me. Who do you think is with Billy?"

Justin began pacing. "The NSA. Hopefully they believe him saying he hasn't seen me."

"Would the National Security Agency test for finger-prints?" Cherie shook her head. "Forget it. Billy's place is such a mess that would take all day."

Justin stopped walking. "Billy said he wouldn't talk, and he won't."

Cherie yawned. "I'm beat after getting up so early and not

sleeping all that great last night. How about we both take a quick nap to recharge, then figure out what to do next?"

Justin eyed the bed. The idea of shutting his eyes was appealing, but he had to stay vigilant. "You go ahead and lie down for a while. I'll keep an eye out."

Cherie nodded and headed to the bed. He watched as she slipped off her shoes and lay down on the mattress, then punched the pillow up and closed her eyes.

Justin went to the window and peered out at the pool below. There were several people sunbathing in the matching lawn chairs. He pulled the curtains shut, casting the room into semi-darkness. He did another quick check on Cherie, who appeared to be sleeping. The place had started to heat up, so he turned on the air conditioner. Then he eyed the couch and considered lying down for a few minutes.

Cherie awoke and opened her eyes to see an unfamiliar clock on a bedside table, the room dark. For a moment, she couldn't remember where she was, then it came flooding back. It was quiet. Had Justin snuck out when she was asleep? She was about to turn on the bedside lamp when she heard movement from the couch. She slid off the bed and walked quietly over, her eyes adjusting in the dark. Justin was lying on his back, asleep, a slight smile on his lips. Cherie suddenly felt the urge to know everything about him. Where did he grow up? Did he have siblings? Why did he join the service in the first place? What she'd seen so far of Justin perplexed her, but—she had to admit—intrigued her.

After Cherie finished dressing and gathering her school-books, Tad still asleep on the other side of the room, she made her way down the hallway. She stopped at Patrick's door and listened. Everything was quiet. She was about to turn the knob, when a voice behind her said, "Did you want something, Cherie?"

Cherie jumped, then turned to face her older brother. "Jeez, Patrick! I was looking for you."

"What did you want?" Shoeless and hair mussed, he appeared to not have slept.

"Are you okay?" she said, abandoning the thought of coercing him into helping with breakfast. She studied his face, his eyes tired.

He hesitated. "I'm fine, baby sis. I just have a big exam today, so I got up early to study."

"Mom's home?" she asked him.

"Yeah, she went to bed a while ago. You're up early."

"I was thinking I'd make pancakes. Tad was asking for some last night."

"What's Tad hoping for, breakfast in bed?" He gave a half smile. "Save me a stack. I'm gonna take a shower."

Cherie nodded as her brother headed into his room. Then she went into the kitchen and opened the fridge, pulling out eggs and milk. When she swung around to set them on the counter, she noticed Patrick's now empty backpack sitting on the kitchen table.

It was evening when Justin finally stirred. At first, he was quiet, then he jumped up suddenly. "What time is it?"

Cherie, who was digging around in her suitcase looking for a snack, glanced at the clock. "Six-thirty."

Justin roughed his hands through his hair. "Thanks for letting me sleep."

"Sure," said Cherie. She located a packet of peanuts and was about to open it when a phone pinged. "That must be yours."

Justin pulled his phone out and checked it. He looked relieved at what he read.

"Good news?" asked Cherie.

He put the phone back in his pocket. "Yes, from Billy. The NSA left."

Just then there was a sharp rapping on the hotel room door.

8

"Room service," called out a man's voice.

"Did you order something?" asked Justin.

Cherie shook her head. She walked over to the door and looked through the peephole to see a man with a cart.

"This must be a mistake," she said through the door. "I didn't order anything."

"That's not what the instructions say, *Señorita*," called the man.

Justin had come up behind her, his body tense. A woman passed by just then and the man turned suddenly and grabbed her. He pulled a gun from under his waiter jacket and put it to her head. "Open up now, or her blood will be on your hands."

At the man's words, Justin peered through the spyhole, then whispered, "Open it." He went into the bathroom and almost closed the door, leaving it slightly ajar.

Cherie cracked the door. Wide-eyed with terror, the woman started to cry out, when the man hissed, "Shut up, or I'll shoot."

"Release her, and I'll let you in," said Cherie.

"One wrong move, and I'll shoot her," he said.

Cherie slowly opened the door, and the man pulled the woman inside with him, kicking the door shut behind them. He pushed the woman toward the couch and ordered, "Sit down and keep your mouth shut."

Then he turned to Cherie, the gun pointed at her chest.

"Who are you, and what do you want?" she said.

"You know what we want." He held the gun steady, his eyes boring into hers.

Cherie waited. When he didn't elaborate, she replied, "I haven't a clue. Enlighten me."

"Stop playing games, Agent Tomlinson."

Cherie studied the man's face, searching her mind for who he could possibly be and what he wanted. When she still didn't respond, fury colored his face scarlet. "Just give me the location."

The woman on the couch began weeping silently.

"Shut up, bitch," he hollered, waving the gun in her direction. The woman grabbed a throw pillow, pressing it against her mouth.

"I'm sure we can work something out," said Cherie. "Just let her go, and I'll see what I can do about getting you the information you want."

"That's not going to happen," the man snarled, then reached out to grab Cherie's arm. Just as he did this, Justin charged out of the bathroom and yanked the man away from her, wrestling the gun from his hand and pressing the weapon against his cheek.

"You don't want to get involved in this," said the man to Justin.

"Too late," Justin said, then smacked him hard on the side of the head with the butt of the gun. The man dropped to the floor, and Justin wiped down the gun and set it next to his body.

Cherie ran to the woman, helping her stand on unsteady feet. "Leave and don't speak to anyone about this. No one, do you hear?" she told her. "Stay in your room and don't answer the door."

The woman nodded, eyes large.

Cherie gave her a brief hug and put her arm around her shoulders as they headed to the door. "You're going to be okay." Then she checked the hallway, and the woman scurried away without looking back.

Cherie ran to grab her suitcase, and they left the room. Justin pointed to the staircase. Once in the stairwell, he said, "I say we make our way to the basement floor and go out where the garage is. If he's working with someone, they probably have the front door covered."

They ran down the stairs, opened the heavy steel door at the bottom, and peered out into a sea of cars. No one. Then they exited the garage and headed toward the beach around the back of the hotel. There was a party going on outside behind the hotel for guests. Music played and a bonfire burned while the smell of barbecue filled the air. "Let's head toward the water," suggested Cherie. "There's no lights out there."

Justin nodded, and they made their way to the shore. When they were a few feet away from the ocean, Cherie reached down to take off her sandals. As the warm water met her feet, she stood for a moment to catch her breath.

Justin stopped and removed his shoes. "Let's go north," he said. "Away from the hotel."

As they walked, the noise of the beach party faded. Then Cherie saw something flash along the shore ahead of them. She stopped and pointed. "There's something up ahead," she whispered. "Maybe a cigarette." It was dark now, the only other light coming from the stars.

"I see it," said Justin. "Let's wait."

As they stood there, a breeze kicked up, and Cherie felt ocean spray coating her face. A few moments later, the hum of a speedboat filled the air. "Get down," said Justin, grabbing her arm and throwing them onto the ground. Cherie dropped next to him, flattening herself as the boat's headlights scudded across the beach.

Cheek pressed against the damp sand, Cherie watched a boat come in and a man run to grab the front of the vessel as the waves kicked up, drenching him with water. Then from the shore came several people. Cherie's heart sped up when she saw an assault rifle in the hands of a person pushing a man and a woman toward the boat.

"Please, don't do this," the woman cried out in English.

The man forcing them forward hit her companion across the head with the rifle, sending him careening onto the sand.

"Oh, my, god," screamed the woman, reaching down to help him up.

"Keep going, or I'll crush his skull next time." The man forced the couple onto the boat as the other man shone the beam of a flashlight across the wide expanse of sand. Cherie held her breath when the light bounced off her and Justin. For a moment, the man stood there, but then the boat's engine roared, and he turned and hoisted himself onto the vessel. As they sped away, the boat bouncing up and down on the waves, the man with the rifle held it aloft. Once they were swallowed up by the night, Cherie whispered, "I think we're safe."

"Let's wait a little longer," said Justin. "They might have left someone behind to check the area." They continued to lay there.

Sure enough, a couple of minutes later, a light sparked near where the boat had left, and the scent of cigarette reached them on the breeze. For a few long minutes, the figure smoked the cigarette, then a phone buzzed. "*Sí,*" said a woman's voice. *"No hay nadie. Está bien, ya voy."* She threw the cigarette on the sand, then turned and walked toward shore, after awhile disappearing into one of the nearby hotels.

Justin peered at Cherie in the moonlight as they both slowly sat up and stood. "You okay?"

Cherie looked back toward the glittering hotel. "That woman's voice. I know it."

9

"It's pretty doubtful you would encounter someone you know here in Mexico," said Justin. "Are you certain?"

Cherie replayed the voice of the woman in her head, trying to recall where she may have heard it. "No, I'm not certain. Probably just a similar tone of voice. Should we keep heading north?"

"That seems the safest. We need to find a place where we can get off the main path and lie low."

"I agree." She felt anxious to find a spot where they could stay hidden from view until morning.

They began walking, Justin periodically checking behind them. She was used to being in dangerous situations with her team, but this unplanned experience with him in the dark—literally and figuratively—had her on edge. Waves crashed on the nearby sand as she took long strides to keep up with him. She glanced at Justin as they walked, his profile resolute. A strong feeling of quiet trust that she hadn't experienced in a long time overtook her.

It was a dark, but starry night. Justin looked up as they walked at a sky flecked with a thousand sparkling pinpoints. He wished he and Cherie could stop and enjoy it, instead of worrying about staying alive. Despite the dangerous circumstances, she continued to walk beside him, her footsteps sure and steady.

"We'll be fine," he said to her suddenly.

Staying in step, she replied, "I'm going to believe that."

When they reached an area where several large boulders sat back from the shore, they stopped. Nature had created a natural space between the rocks where they settled themselves on the sand, able to see down the beach, but hidden from view.

"Man, I'm hungry," Justin said, leaning back on his elbows.

Cherie rummaged in her suitcase, then handed him a small bag of nuts. "I always come prepared." She laughed.

He looked at the provisions with surprise. "I'd pay you ten bucks for this right now," he said, ripping the bag open and pouring half of the nuts into her open palm. Then he shook the remaining contents into his mouth, crunching the nuts noisily.

Cherie yawned. "Just so we don't die."

"I won't let that happen." Justin meant those words, surprised at how protective he felt of her. "How about you close your eyes for a few? I'll keep watch."

Cherie tried to make herself comfortable on the sand. She lay down and put her head on her suitcase, positioning herself where she could see all the way to the water, determined to not be taken unaware. Her body felt heavy with fatigue, and yet, she couldn't get comfortable enough to fall asleep. Finally, she sat up. "You said you were framed. What happened exactly? We've come this far together, and I really want to know."

Justin was silent for a time, a look on his face as if he wanted to tell her everything. But then he closed the subject. "If you don't know, you'll have deniability. I'd rather keep it that way. Try to sleep."

Frustration surged through Cherie as she lay her head back on her suitcase. She knew he was right. The legality of not knowing protected her to some measure. But it had begun to eat at her. She was never good with unanswered questions. Secrets and half-truths bothered her. It had always been that way.

"Patrick, where are you going?" Cherie had heard her brother leave his room. It was past midnight, and he was at the front door, his hand on the doorknob.

"Just out for a bite to eat."

"It's the middle of the night. You're going alone?"

"McDonalds is twenty-four hours," he said. "A friend might meet me there. What do you want? I'll bring you back something."

Cherie eyed him, noting he carried his backpack. "Why do you need your backpack?"

"I've got it packed for school tomorrow. I'm just going to leave it in the car."

"My, aren't you organized. Doesn't exactly sound like you. Where are you really going, Patrick?" Cherie knew he was lying but wasn't about to come clean with her; he never did. "Get me an apple and cherry pie. I'll wait up for you."

His brows furrowed in a frown. "Go to bed. I'll be fine." He turned the doorknob.

"When are you coming back?" she said to his back.

"In a little while."

Her brother left the house, the door clicking behind him. She went to the window, hearing the car start up and then saw it pull out of the driveway. When he was gone, she went to sit on the couch to wait. For a time, she stayed awake, believing he would be right back, like he said. But when a half hour turned into an hour, she dozed off. At dawn, she opened her eyes to see two pies on the coffee table.

Cherie smiled, happy Patrick was home. But then she wondered once again, where was her brother going in the middle of the night?

Cherie finally fell asleep to the rhythmic sound of the

waves sliding onto shore. Her slumber was fitful and uncomfortable, and it was still dark when she woke to find Justin awake staring at the sea. She brushed sand from her cheeks and sat up. "I'm awake if you want to get some sleep."

Justin didn't say anything for a moment. Finally, he nodded.

"You can use my suitcase for a pillow."

"It's okay. I can sleep sitting up." He leaned against a boulder.

"That's a skill I haven't acquired, but whatever works," said Cherie, scanning their surroundings. Justin closed his eyes, and his shoulders soon slumped. As she stood watch, she thought about next steps. Her flight left in the morning, but she doubted she'd be able to make it. The best thing for her to do at this point would be to call her boss at the FBI and explain what was going on. But what would she say? That she was on the run with someone who was AWOL? Her boss would likely urge her to come home. And what about the couple they saw being held against their will? If American tourists were being kidnapped, Cherie had to find out what was going on.

When the horizon lightened, Justin opened his eyes and stretched his neck and shoulders. "Not a bad sleep," he said. "But I wouldn't want to spend another night here."

"That couldn't have been restful," said Cherie. She shook sand out of her hair.

"You were able to stay awake." Justin sounded impressed. "We better get moving again before somebody shows up."

The morning air was chilly, and Cherie's clothes felt damp from the early mist. She trembled, wrapping her arms around herself.

"You're cold," said Justin, scooting closer and pulling her to him.

At first, she stiffened, surprised by his action.

"Relax," he said, and lightly stroked her hair. "You need to warm up a little, okay? The sun will be up before long."

She nodded and let her body sink into his warmness.

"Maybe we'll run across some food," he said. "Hot coffee sounds terrific right now, doesn't it?"

"Heavenly," said Cherie, leaning into him, enjoying the feeling of their bodies pressed together.

After a few minutes of watching the sky lighten as seagulls swooped in to peck in the wet sand, Cherie said reluctantly, "We probably should get going."

As they began walking, Justin pointed straight ahead. "There's a marina soon. I'm thinking we rent a boat to hole up on and figure out what to do next. Maybe we just drift down the coast for a while."

"I don't have much experience with boats," said Cherie.

"Believe it or not, I have a boating license. My father insisted on it. You're safe with me."

"Where'd you learn?" Cherie expected Justin to skirt the question, but he answered.

"My father first, and then more training in the Marines."

"So, it's the Marines you're running from," she said. "How old were you when your father taught you to drive a boat?"

"Sixteen, seventeen. We lived in California at the time. We'd take deep-sea fishing trips off the coast."

Cherie pictured Justin out at sea as a teenager pulling up giant fish.

They soon came upon the marina, still quiet in the dawn hour.

"I don't see a rental office." She looked at the cloudless blue sky. "At least the weather is holding."

"It's a little more informal here," said Justin. Cherie noticed two men heading from shore making their way toward the dock. One carried a fishing net and the other a cooler.

"*Hola,*" called out Justin. The men stopped, eyeing them warily.

"*Necesitamos un barco para rentar. Tenemos* cash," said Justin.

The men looked at each other, then one said, "You want to rent a boat, talk to Geraldo. He's there, in the catamaran."

Cherie and Justin headed down the dock, stopping at a blue catamaran with the name Esmerelda painted on the side. A man stood on deck tending a small smoking grill on which clams cooked. He was short and muscular and wore a baseball cap sideways on his head and swimming trunks.

"Geraldo?" Justin asked.

The man gave them a tentative smile. "*Sí?*"

"We hear you're the man to talk to about renting a boat."

His smiled widened. "*Sí, sí.*" He motioned for them to climb aboard.

"We'd like something like this for a few days. We can pay cash," said Justin.

"This boat is two-thousand pesos a day, and you need to pay before you leave the dock."

"We can do that in US dollars," said Justin.

The man nodded in approval. "That is okay. You need to get the boat back in five days before the owners return."

Cherie spoke up. "This isn't your boat?"

"I take care of it. Don't worry, *Señorita*, it's okay."

Cherie looked around at the boats docked nearby—Voyager, Sunshine, Princess. She wondered if this was such a good idea.

10

When Cherie didn't say anything more, Justin finished counting out the money and handed it to the man, who grinned and pushed it into his pants pocket.

"Come, I show you where everything is," he said.

Twenty minutes later, after getting a tour of the catamaran, a rundown of the day's weather, and filling up the gas tanks, they headed out of the marina into the open water. By now dawn had turned to morning. As Cherie sat and watched Justin steer the boat, she shook her head to clear it. Was this all some crazy dream, and she'd eventually wake up? All she could hope for now was the owners didn't have the coast guard chase the boat down and arrest the two of them. Cherie had a lot of explaining to do when she saw her boss, Savannah. She didn't need to add a bigger chain of events to what was already overload. Suddenly, a dolphin rose out of the water near the boat, the water sliding off its sleek body. Cherie squealed, amazed to see something so wonderful. The creature jumped several more times, as if showing off, then disappeared. If only they could stay out at sea for days and days with nothing to fear or worry about. But that was just wishful thinking.

"Do you think the man who rented us the boat is really in charge of watching over it?"

Justin checked some gauges as he steered. "Probably, although I doubt the owners know he's renting it out and getting paid double. Times are tough here. What I just paid him can feed his family for months."

"So, we're doing a good deed stealing a boat?"

Justin chuckled. "If you put it that way, yes."

Cherie gazed across the water, her eyes seeing miles of blue sea. Seagulls flew overhead, squawking and diving down to skim the water's surface while whitecaps danced beneath them. There was something about being out here on the water that gradually calmed her. She had promised Justin she could figure any problem out. Maybe it was a good idea to get away from the land and its many minefields. She thought about the conversation with the man in the hotel room and his reference to wanting a location. For what?

"Do you think there is reception out here?" she asked.

"We're still pretty close to land, so probably. Why?"

"I need to call my boss about what the man in the hotel room said. And about the couple that was kidnapped."

Justin's jaw tightened. "What else are you going to tell her?"

Cherie was silent for a moment. "She's going to want to know where I am."

Justin looked at her pointedly. "Where are you?"

Cherie pushed her hair out of her face. What would she say to Savannah that would make sense? Her boss was shrewd. She'd know something else was up. But Cherie had also learned from personal experience that not saying anything had its own dangers.

"Cherie, where is your brother?"

"Tad's in the bedroom getting dressed for school."

"I'm talking about Patrick."

Cherie's mom had just gotten home. She leaned against the kitchen counter and slipped out of her nursing shoes, reaching down to rub a foot.

"He wasn't in his room?" Cherie took a sip of orange juice to soothe the knot of worry in her throat about Patrick.

"No, I don't see him anywhere. Have you noticed that he's been acting odd lately?"

Cherie put on a poker face. "Odd? I don't think so. Why?" Her mother's words added to her mounting concerns about her brother and his mysterious late-night activities.

"You can't tell me you haven't noticed. You're here with him more than me. Is there something going on with him?" Her mother opened the fridge and took out the orange juice, then poured herself a glass.

Cherie thought about the backpack that mysteriously filled then emptied.

"Cherie?" her mother said. "What are you not telling me?"

To her relief, Tad straggled in. "I made you PB and J for lunch," she told her little brother. She combed through his mussed hair with her fingers. He responded by wrinkling his nose and protesting. "I already brushed my hair, and I want marshmallow creme on bread." Tad held a Tupperware containing his latest pet, a spider named Marvin.

Cherie glanced at the clock on the wall. "I've got to get Tad to the bus stop, Mom."

Her mother sighed. "I'm going to bed. You both have a good day at school."

Cherie swallowed, her head spinning with concern over Patrick. Her brother always came home before their mother did. Where was he?

Cherie stood and stumbled as the catamaran shifted on a wave. She pulled her cellphone out of her pocket, then gripped a railing. "I'll be right here when I make the call," she told him.

Justin shrugged his shoulders as Cherie called Savannah. She expected her boss to pick up on the first couple of rings like she usually did, but the call went to voicemail. She pocketed her phone and sat back down.

They continued on for some time as the sun rose higher in the sky. At one point, Cherie felt her stomach rumble. "I'm going to go below deck and see what there is to eat in the kitchen."

It felt good to be out on the ocean, but Justin knew this was a temporary reprieve. Shading his eyes, he could see what might be a rise of land in the distance. There was a string of small islands out here. They'd have to dock at some point to conserve fuel. He knew he should be worried about Cherie being FBI, but somehow, he trusted her.

"Look what I found," she said when she came up from below deck holding a can of Spam and another of corn. "Want me to cook it up? I'm starving."

"Go for it." He watched her, midday sun golden on her skin, her hair shifting in the wind. She looked happy, excited to have found something for them to eat. It was as if they had embarked on a journey to some far-off land, and she was in charge of overseeing rations. He laughed to himself.

"Do you have to stay at the wheel the whole time? I mean, do we eat in shifts?" she asked him.

"I can anchor. Do you need help in the kitchen?" The idea of being close to Cherie in a tight space held a certain appeal.

She put a hand on a hip. "I think I can handle this gourmet feast. How about I bring up two plates when it's done?"

Justin smiled. "I'd like that."

A few minutes later, Cherie came back with the food and a bottle of something under her arm.

"Is that alcohol?" he asked hopefully.

Cherie set the plates on the deck and pulled the bottle out from under her arm with a flourish. "A bottle of red wine I found in one of the cupboards. Hopefully they haven't been saving it for a special occasion."

"This is a special occasion," said Justin as he stopped the engine.

A ripple of pleasure raced through Cherie at Justin's

words. *A special occasion*. She glanced at the horizon in the afternoon sun, noting how the azure skyline disappeared into the sea. Then she watched in appreciation as Justin's arm muscles contracted when he cranked the boat's anchor.

"Let's sit on the deck," he said when he finished, then headed to the front. After opening a few compartments, he pulled out a small table and two chairs, setting it all up quickly.

Cherie put the plates on the table, along with two glasses, then handed him the bottle. "I couldn't find a corkscrew."

"That would be the worst thing I could imagine," he said. "Out at sea with a bottle of good wine and no way to open it. We need to remedy that."

Justin pulled off the foil capsule around the top of the bottle, then set it on the table. He yanked open another compartment and began rooting around until he found an icepick. Sitting down on a chair, he put the bottle between his knees and inserted the pick into the cork, then worked it out of the bottle. When the cork came out with a ruby stain, he shouted, "Success!"

Cherie laughed and held out the glasses for him to fill. A warm feeling existed between them, more relaxed now that they were out of harm for the moment. She realized that until then she had hardly seen him smile. She must have had an odd expression on her face, because he stopped, the bottle in midair. "What is it?" He looked out at the ocean. "Did you see something?"

"No. Everything's fine." She laid a hand on his arm. "I was just thinking how nice it is to see you smile. It's sweet." She felt suddenly self-conscious at her words.

Justin paused for a moment, then began pouring more wine. "I could tell you the smile is because you found alcohol for us to drink." He finished topping off the glasses. "But I would be lying."

11

Cherie lifted her glass of wine. "Should we toast to something?"

Justin reached his glass toward hers. "To what is hopefully good wine on a gorgeous day with a beautiful woman."

Cherie felt her face flush as they tapped their glasses together. Unable to think of the right thing to say, she smiled and took a sip of the wine, which was incredibly good.

When Justin took a swallow, he lifted the bottle and read the label. "Calera, a 2018 Pinot Noir from California. Has an amazing taste." He set down the glass and picked up a fork, then speared a piece of Spam. After chewing a mouthful, he said, "This is pretty good for canned meat."

"I used to cook this for my brothers," she said, sinking her fork tines into her own piece.

"Brothers? You mentioned one brother before."

Cherie chewed and swallowed. "Two brothers. One older. His name is Patrick, and then there is Tadpole, and he's the youngest. His real name is Thomas, but we've called him Tadpole, or Tad, since he was tiny."

"Like a tailed larvae?"

"Exactly. He was always trying to squiggle out of our arms when he was a baby."

"Where do your brothers live?"

"Tad lives in New Jersey with my mother. He's attending Rutgers."

"That's a good school. What's he studying?"

Cherie smiled. "Biology. Ever since he was a little kid, he has loved animals. What about your family? Any siblings?"

Justin had cleared his plate and took another sip of wine. "A sister, Collette, and my folks."

"Where do they live?"

"My old man lives in Maryland. My mom is in Southern California. They're divorced. And then Collette is in Montana. She met and married a cowboy." Justin poured more wine into his glass and held the bottle up. "More?"

Cherie nodded.

"So, what made you become an FBI agent?"

Cherie pushed her hair behind her ears. "The job kind of found me. I was about to graduate from high school and had been accepted to a few universities. Then I met Savannah, my boss, at a family friend's retirement party. When she told me she was an agent—I don't know. Something just clicked. We talked for a while, especially about CSI, which is her specialty, and I decided once I had my undergraduate degree that I would apply."

"Isn't it hard to be accepted?"

"They only take about twenty percent of applicants. What about you? How did you end up in the military?"

"My father. He's retired Navy. Now he works as a consultant."

"Oh."

"Yeah, oh," said Justin. "I hear your next question. Why doesn't he help me with my current predicament?"

"I was thinking that."

Justin set down his glass. "Because he might be involved."

"That's a pretty big statement."

"And a pretty big problem."

They sat in silence for a time, the boat moving up and down in the waves, the sails making a flapping sound in the breeze. Justin finally spoke. "You asked what happened."

Cherie shifted in her seat to face him.

Justin's jaws tightened, one hand clenching into a fist. He stood up and fixed his eyes in the distance, a concerned look on his face. "That boat tearing through the water is heading straight for us," he said. "We better pull up the anchor and get moving. It could be nothing, but right now we're sitting dead in the water."

Cherie shot up from her chair. "What do you want me to do?"

Justin ran starboard and began cranking the anchor. "Secure the dishes and hang on."

Justin headed east, away from their potential visitors. "Come back here," he told Cherie.

"They're getting closer," she called out as she crossed the deck.

"It looks like the Mexican coast guard," said Justin. The boat neared then and an alarm sounded.

"I think they're pulling us over," said Cherie, her tone anxious.

As the boat approached—the name *Búsqueda y Rescate Marítimo* on the side of the vessel—a man with a blowhorn called out, *"Buenas tardes, Señor y Señora."*

"*Buenas tardes,*" Justin called out.

"*A dónde van todos?*" The man asked where they were going.

"*Aquí y allá,*" said Justin, telling the man that they were just out and about.

"*Tienen ustedes papeles de registro y identificación?*"

"He wants to see our registration and identification," said Justin.

"What are we going to do?"

The boats were now nearly touching. "*Puedo pasar?*" said the man with the blowhorn.

Justin waved him onboard.

"You're telling him to board?" Cherie gasped as the vessels tapped and the man, tall and thin and dressed in a red uniform with yellow stripes, climbed on their boat.

"*Un problema,*" said Justin to the man once he was onboard. "We seem to have misplaced our registration."

"That is a problem," said the man, his eyes darting about as he spoke. He looked at Cherie and then back at Justin. "This is your vessel, *Señor?*"

"The paperwork is back home. We just decided to come down to the dock and take a leisurely ride on the water. You know, break the boredom. I guess we weren't thinking."

"And where is home? You are American?"

"Yes," said Justin.

"There are penalties here in Mexico for not having your registration," said the man.

"Are penalties something we can deal with?" asked Justin. He reached a hand into his pocket and let it rest there. When the man didn't object, only nodded, Justin pulled out a roll of bills. "I hope this will cover things?"

The man glanced back at his boat, then took the money. "I need to inspect your vessel to ensure that it is safe."

Justin let the man pass. He went below deck while he and

Cherie waited. When she looked as if she might have questions, Justin shook his head in a quick no. The man emerged from below, a broad smile on his face. "All looks according to code," he exclaimed, taking ahold of Justin's hand and giving it a hearty shake. "Have a good day." Then he disembarked and ordered his crew away from their boat.

"That looked like a lot of cash," said Cherie.

"It was just about all I had, but it bought us some time."

"Do you think he'll report us, even though you gave him a bribe?"

"If the right people offer the right price, yes."

12

"We need to find an island where we can dock and lie low for awhile," said Justin, checking the skyline. "If my memory serves me correctly, there is a string of isles farther out in the Pacific."

Never in a zillion years did Cherie expect her vacation would take such a turn. But as Justin shifted the boat into high gear, she felt a whoosh of excitement. You wanted to shake up your world, she thought. Waves slapped against the sides of the boat, a spray of water coming over the sides. She held fast to the rail, lowering her head against the wind, her hair streaming behind her.

Some time passed, and a green oasis in the blue water came into view. Justin slowed the boat and asked Cherie, "Can you check around for some binoculars?"

Cherie remembered seeing a pair hanging in the kitchen. She ran down to retrieve them.

Justin stopped the boat and took the binoculars out on deck to survey the island.

"Anything?" she called.

"I think so," he said, returning to the cabin. "Ready to check it out?"

Cherie laughed. "Now you're asking me if I'm ready?"

Justin gave her a small smile. "I know things have been moving fast. I'm sorry to have gotten you into this mess."

"Technically," said Cherie, "it was me who got you involved when those men tried to grab me at the airport. We're both in trouble right now. A remote island seems like a good place to stop and figure out what's what."

Justin thrummed his fingers on the helm. "Okay, hold tight." The engine revved and water churned around the boat.

A few minutes later, they approached the island, covered in dense forest. Justin slowed down, and she picked up the binoculars to study the landscape. No signs of human life. When they were close, Justin said, "I'm looking for an inlet." At that moment, a great white bird lifted from the island, another following close behind, their beauty astonishing Cherie. "Over there." She pointed. "I see an indentation along the shoreline."

When they came to the inlet, Justin slowed the boat to a crawl. "Take the helm for me," he said. "I need to make sure it's not too shallow before we go in."

Cherie took over, gripping the steering wheel and eyeing the controls, unsure of what to do. "Is this like a car?"

"Pretty much."

Justin dug in one of the compartments on deck and pulled out a long pole. He began dragging it through the water to measure the water's depth and check for rocks. It appeared deep enough. He surveyed the inlet with its small, deserted beach.

"Cherie," he called.

She stuck her head out of the cabin.

"I need you to come keep an eye out for rocks, or anything floating. I'm going to go in really slow. Just shout if anything comes up suddenly."

Cherie saluted when Justin came back to the cabin. "Aye, aye captain."

Justin shook his head. "You have a great way of lightening a taxing situation." He studied her for a moment. "That's a real gift."

Cherie didn't answer, instead grew serious as she took up post surveying the water. She gave him the okay sign as he maneuvered the catamaran into the cove, soon easing the front of the boat onto a lip of soft sand. He got out some rope and coiled it around a metal cleat on deck, then tossed the other end onshore. After hopping out, he tied the rope to a banyan tree.

"It's lovely here," said Cherie, who stood on deck, looking out at the beach, the island lush and green in the late afternoon sun.

Justin waded over to her. "Let me help you down," he said, reaching up to take her by the waist before she could reply and hoisting her over the railing and into the warm water with him.

Cherie took in a surprised breath, her blue eyes on his.

Justin brushed back a lock of hair from her cheek, and they stood there for a moment, neither saying anything as the warm water lapped around them.

"It's quiet here," said Cherie, her voice barely above a whisper.

Justin moved closer. "You're beautiful." He leaned down

and took her mouth in his. The kiss was long and slow, and Justin felt his own arousal. When they finished, he murmured, "I've wanted to do that since we met."

Cherie pulled her head back, a surprised expression on her face. "You did?"

Justin smiled and shook his head slightly. "You don't know how gorgeous you are, do you?" It was a statement more than a question.

All of a sudden, Cherie shrieked and pulled away. "There's something in the water!"

Justin looked down to see a fish swimming around her ankles as she lifted one leg, then another. He reached out and lifted her off the shallow ocean floor and carried her to the sandy shore.

"What was it?" she asked.

"It was just a fish." He lowered her to the sand, then sat down next to her.

"Just a fish? It took me off guard." Her face flushed a charming shade of pink.

"Did me kissing you take you off guard?"

"No, yes, I mean." She pushed her hair away from her face.

Justin waited.

"Maybe a little," she said finally.

They sat for a time as the water lapped onshore. Justin watched a seagull dive into the water and snap up a fish. "Did you know that seagulls mate for life?" he said, turning to look at her.

Cherie picked up a handful of sand and let it slip through her fingertips. "No, I didn't."

"The other gulls in the colony will gang up on predators, too, if something tries to attack one of their own."

Cherie took another handful of sand. "More interesting facts."

"I minored in marine biology."

"Where did you grow up?"

"Southern California." He reached forward to snag a small rock and threw it into the water.

Cherie dug her toes into the sand. "I lived in California when I was young on base. Camp Pendleton. My mom is from Jersey, so we moved back when my father died. I don't remember too much. What was it like growing up there?"

"Sunny, hot a lot of the time. The people are friendly. The food is good."

"Your mother still lives there. Do you visit her often?" asked Cherie.

Justin picked up another beach stone and turned it over in his hands. "No, I haven't seen her in a few years."

"Is that by choice?" asked Cherie, then stopped herself. "I'm sorry, I'm prying. Forget I asked."

"It's okay. My parents' breakup was ugly. I was in my first year of college when they split. My mother got remarried very quickly. It was all so awkward, I just distanced myself. I didn't know what to say to either of them, I guess."

"I'm sorry," said Cherie. "That sounds like it was tough."

Justin liked the way Cherie listened without judgment and somehow understood. "I'll tell you why I'm AWOL," he said.

13

When Justin said he was going to tell her why he was on the run, Cherie set down the shell she'd been admiring and waited.

He looked out at the sea, his gaze focused on something only he could see. "I graduated top of my class in high school. I was the valedictorian. My main interest at the time was computers. I even considered becoming a video game developer. But my father, as I mentioned, was in the Navy, so he was always on me to join the service. It was his idea that I use my computer skills and go into cryptology."

Justin stopped for a moment and shifted in the sand. "I enlisted and took the training and did well with it. I got all the upper-level security clearance. I was also trained in combat, so I could go into enemy territory, if need be, and protect myself. I did well with that, too. For a while, I was the golden boy. And my father couldn't have been prouder. Then last November I was sent into a situation in Africa. Sudan. Though the US has an agreement that the country won't become a haven for terrorists, there were some questions as to if that was occurring."

Cherie waited while he paused, then spoke up. "Was it occurring?"

"I used all my cryptology skills and found nothing, but I stumbled onto something else. The US gives a tremendous amount of aid to the country, but I discovered some was being diverted to a shell corporation in Belize. I brought back the information to my superiors, and I was told they would take care of it and given another assignment. When I didn't see anything happening about Sudan, I asked about its status and was told to just leave it alone. It was then that I went to my father. He also told me in no uncertain terms to forget about it. I probably should have, but I'd been to the country. I'd seen the want and need there, and I couldn't help thinking about how the aid should be going to the people, not to line someone's pockets. I guess I can't help but rock the boat sometimes."

"I admire that," said Cherie. "I've always had a hard time rocking the boat. Even when the boat needs to be turned upside down."

Justin gave her a wry smile. "I have to admit I was reeling, wondering if my father was involved. Soon after, I discovered my phone had been bugged. Then the morning of the day we flew here, someone deposited a large sum of money into an account I haven't used in a while."

"How much?"

"Five-hundred-thousand dollars."

Cherie whistled. "Yikes."

"I happened to discover the deposit right away. I knew it was only a matter of hours until they came to arrest me, so I bolted. I went straight to Dulles, figuring I'd get on the soonest flight out. Since Billy is here, and he's the only one I trusted to tell about this, I decided to come here." He stopped and glanced at Cherie. "When I saw you sitting next to me in the café, I was panicked. I needed to act normal, all the while trying to figure out my next step. I'm sorry. I must have terri-fied you, but I had run out of options. I had to get on that flight."

Cherie looked at him. "I was terrified and unsure of what was going on, or what you might do next. The only thing was, though, you seemed like you wouldn't harm me. I don't know how I knew that, but I did." She shook her head. "You didn't even have a gun. What kind of bad guy is that?"

"So now that you know my predicament, any ideas?"

Cherie thought for a moment. "You should start by checking out everyone involved and ruling people out. Elim-ination. That will help give you the clarity you need."

Justin nodded. "If I could get ahold of some good equip-ment—an encrypted laptop ideally—I could do just that."

"I've got the laptop, but I'm not sure we have internet access out here."

"I saw a satellite receiver in the cabin," said Justin. Then he looked back at the island behind them.

"Do you think the island is uninhabited?" she asked.

"We can't know for certain. I think we need to be cautious."

"You know, I could check in with my boss. She might be able to help with this."

Justin shook his head. "You can't involve anyone else."

"We need someone's help. You trust Billy. I trust Savannah."

Justin was quiet for a moment. "Okay. You can probably make a call using VoIP on the computer."

Back on the boat, they were able to connect the computer to satellite, and Cherie made the call. Savannah's phone rang and voicemail picked up immediately. "Let me try the lab," she said, almost to herself. Someone answered on the first ring. "Garcia speaking."

"Hi Jasmine, it's Cherie. I'm looking for Savannah."

"Cherie! How's Mexico? God, I so envy you. It's snowing here."

"It's great. I've got something I really need to talk to Savannah about."

"She left on some hush-hush assignment. The call came from the higher-ups."

"Any idea when you might hear from her?"

"Sorry, no. Anything I can do?"

Cherie was about to hang up, then said, "Maybe there is. I'm hearing about people going missing here in Mexico. Americans. Would you mind having Violet investigate and see what she can dig up?"

"Sure. In the meantime, try to relax and have fun. Have a margarita for me."

Cherie laughed. "Deal. My cell doesn't work all that well here. Have Violet send me an email."

When she hung up, Cherie said, "That's odd."

"What?"

"I've worked for Savannah for six years. She has never been called away on mysterious, undisclosed business."

14

"If you're worried about your boss, I can hack into the Bureau and see if there is a paper trail," offered Justin.

"Let me think about it. Don't you have some other hacking to do?"

Justin frowned.

"Are you afraid of what you're going to find when you access your father's emails?"

He gave her a sidelong glance. "Does it show?"

"I've had my own family stuff, believe me." Cherie looked out at the waning day. It would be sunset soon, and then night would close in.

A loud knocking awoke Cherie, who had fallen asleep

reading her geology book on the living room couch. She sat up, finally registering that the pounding was coming from the front door. Did Patrick forget his key, she wondered as she went to the door. When she looked through the peephole, her heart flip-flopped to see two policemen standing on the front porch.

"What is it?" she called out.

"This is the Trenton police. Please open the door."

Cherie cracked the door, blinking from the porch light's glare. "What happened?"

"Is there a Patrick Tomlinson here?"

Cherie glanced behind her, then at the policemen. "Patrick is my brother. I don't know if he's here."

"May we come in?" said one officer.

Cherie pulled her robe tighter, then stepped back and let them in.

"I'll go check his room." She hurried down the hallway and flung open Patrick's door, praying he would be inside. No one. She checked the bathroom. Empty. Then she peeked in on Tad, who was thankfully still asleep.

She returned to the officers standing in the doorway. "He doesn't seem to be home."

"It's three in the morning. Is he usually out this late?" asked one of the officers.

"Sometimes. He falls asleep doing homework at his girlfriend's," she added quickly.

"You're Patrick's sister?"

Cherie nodded.

"Is a parent home?"

Cherie swallowed. "My mother isn't in right now."

"How old are you?"

Cherie thought about lying but decided that wouldn't be wise. "Fourteen."

"Are you usually alone at night?"

"Patrick is usually here. He's eighteen. My mom comes home at six in the morning. She works the nightshift as a nurse."

"And what about your father?"

Cherie looked down at her bare feet, then back up again. "He died fighting in Afghanistan."

The officer who asked about her father glanced at the other man, then addressed Cherie. "We'll be back in the morning to speak to your mother. And we need to talk to your brother as soon as possible. Any problems, give us a call."

"I think I found something," said Justin. "I've been looking at my father's superiors' emails around the time I got back from Sudan."

Cherie leaned over his shoulder to check out the correspondence on the screen. "It looks like it's in some form of code."

"I can translate it," he said. "Just give me a minute." Cherie watched, fascinated, as he hit keys, then opened a document and made notations and numerical calculations, entering more data.

"So, this is what cryptologists do."

"Part of what we do," said Justin, his brow furrowed as he worked. He smiled then. "I've got it. From Commander Taylor to an undisclosed recipient. It says, *Target identified. Tailwind expected. Wait for instructions. Neutralizing necessary.*"

"Does that mean anything to you?" Cherie asked him.

Justin sat back. "I'm not sure about the tailwind reference."

Cherie tapped her foot. "Tailwinds are usually good things, right? Like when you're sailing, they push you along."

"But they can push you along too fast," said Justin.

"True. The real question is, who is the target?"

"I'll have to dig some more," he said.

Cherie stood. "I saw some cans of chili in the cupboard downstairs. I'm going to heat them up and get us something to drink."

When Cherie left, Justin studied his computer screen and read the last line again. *Neutralizing necessary.* He couldn't help wonder if the target was him. He checked the date of the email. Right around the time he reported his findings from Sudan.

He noticed the darkening sky and thought that if he had to be holed up somewhere, this place would certainly do. Though he'd been hesitant to tell Cherie what had happened, he now felt lighter, less burdened. There was something to be said for having a confidante. Justin had never experienced that before.

"Can you come here?" Cherie called from below.

He jumped up and descended the stairs into the kitchen to find Cherie balancing two bowls of chili. "I can't get that top door unlatched. It seems to be stuck. I was hoping I'd find more food up there."

"Let me," he said, reaching up to work the latch of a wide

cupboard. When he got it unlatched, he said, "I think it was rusted shut." He lifted the door and reached in, pulling down a rifle.

Cheri's breath caught. "Is it loaded?"

Justin opened the chamber. "A few rounds."

"I hope we don't need it, but it's good to know we have a weapon. Nothing else up there?"

Justin took down a bottle. "Tequila. Looks like the good stuff, too."

Cherie headed for the stairs. "Grab some cups and spoons."

Once on deck, they sat to face the water and began eating. Justin made an appreciative groan as he ate. "This is really good," he said between mouthfuls. "I didn't realize how hungry I was."

Cherie took a bite and chewed. "I think it's the best chili I've ever had."

Once they'd emptied their bowls, Justin uncorked the tequila and poured the equivalent of two shots into each glass, then handed one to Cherie. He drank his in one long gulp. Cherie took a small drink. She held the glass up. "That's very smooth. It's good," she said, sipping it slowly.

They sat in silence for a time, then Cherie spoke up. "It's so quiet out here. I know I should be more concerned about our predicament, but somehow sitting here in the middle of who knows where, I'm not."

Justin stretched his legs out and stared up at the starry sky. "It's probably the tequila talking, but I'm not either."

"Maybe I've just gotten tired of waiting for the other shoe to drop," said Cherie thoughtfully.

Justin turned to look at her, then she met his eyes in the twilight. He waited for her to continue but she didn't, so he filled the silence. "That's a feeling I can identify with. Is that what you've experienced working for the Bureau?"

"It's a feeling I've had just about my whole life." Cherie sighed. "It started on my sixth birthday, when I found out my father died in Afghanistan."

15

At the sadness in Cherie's voice, something deep inside Justin surfaced. He wanted to do something, give her comfort, make the pain disappear. He reached out and took her hand in his. "I'm sorry you lost your father like that," he said quietly. "That must have been really rough."

Cherie looked out at the dark night, then back at Justin. "It was hardest on Patrick. As the oldest, he thought he had to take care of everything and everyone." The pain in Cherie's eyes when she mentioned her brother was palpable.

"Tell me about Patrick," said Justin.

Cherie had twined her fingers in his. She took a deep breath before tears began welling in her eyes, then spilled down both cheeks. "My mother and Tad won't talk about him anymore."

"I'll listen."

"Mom always said he looked just like my father. He was very handsome. All the girls at school wanted to be invited over to my house in hopes of catching his attention. He wanted to follow in my father's footsteps and join the service." She wiped tears from her face with the fingers of her free hand.

"You said was. Did something happen to him?"

Cherie pressed her lips together. "It's a long story."

"We've got time. Go on. Unless you don't want to."

Cherie took a deep breath. "I do want to talk about what happened. As I said, my brother felt he had to take the role of man of the house. My mother worked nights as a nurse, but there was never enough money. Patrick did odd jobs to help pay the bills, until..." Cherie stopped, her chin trembled. Justin waited.

"I knew something was up. He'd have his backpack filled, and then he'd leave in the night, and the next morning it'd be empty. One night the police came to find him but he wasn't there. They wanted to question him regarding a robbery at an all-night gas station. There was video of a person robbing the place wearing a ski mask. It quickly became clear from what the police said to my mother that they were ready to pin it on Patrick. They asked her if he'd come into any large sums of money recently. He had given her a few thousand dollars to fix the car."

"You don't think it was him robbing the gas station?"

Cherie shook her head. "When I was in training at Quantico, I started looking into what was going on in Trenton at the time in terms of crime. From what I pieced together, Patrick was likely running contraband for a local Italian crime family. Once I became an agent, I was able to obtain the footage of the robbery at the gas station. I know my brother, and the masked man wasn't him. There was also corruption at the police station. My theory is that the Mariano family wanted to protect whoever committed the robbery, so they used my brother as a fall guy."

"What happened to Patrick?"

Cherie shrugged her shoulders. "He just vanished."

"When was that?"

"Ten years ago, this month. My mother is convinced he's dead. But I think he's alive and in hiding."

Justin studied her face. "Where?"

Cherie didn't answer for a few moments. "Here. In Mexico."

"So, this was more than a pleasure trip for you?"

"I had intended on vacationing, but I figured I'd also do some checking around."

"I want to help you find him."

Cherie's eyes filled with hope. "I just need to know he's okay. And—," her voice caught, "to let him know that I never stopped looking for him."

"I can't imagine how painful it must be to wonder what happened to someone you love," said Justin. "If he's here, I'll help you find him. That's a promise."

Cherie leaned over and hugged Justin hard around the neck, burying her face in his chest. When the tears started again, she let go of him and wiped them away. "Thanks for listening," she said. "Most people avoid talking about it when the subject of my brother being missing comes up. Even some of his old friends, people he grew up with. Maybe they're afraid to upset me. But what hurts the most is forgetting him. As if the answer is to pretend like he never existed." She took the last sip of her drink and set the glass on the deck. "Enough of that. I'll be okay. I have to be."

They sat in silence for a while. Then, to lighten the mood, Justin said, "Dance with me."

Cherie gave him a funny look. "There's no music."

He stood and reached out his hand. "We both need to relax and forget things in front of us for now. We can dance to the sound of the water."

Justin's heart lightened when Cherie laughed and replied, "I did plan to dance while I was in Mexico." She accepted his hand, and he pulled her up and took her in his arms. As he buried his face in her silky hair and began to hum, he realized that he wanted this to be more than an accidental meeting. There was something about Cherie that seeped into the core of him, warm and lasting. Overcome with an emotion he was afraid to express, he pulled her even closer as they swayed in unison, the moon casting its silvery glow onto the deck.

Perhaps it was the way Justin listened when she spoke, never taking his eyes from hers. Or the feel of his hands as they held firm around her waist while they danced. A strong desire for him began to overwhelm Cherie, burning in her in a way she had never expected. Her breath caught in her throat, a tremor going through her as she tried to calm her emotions. What was happening to her? Suddenly, she pulled away.

Justin didn't ask what was wrong. It was as if he knew. Silently, he stepped toward her and rested his cheek against hers. "Cherie," he whispered her name, warm in her ear, creating goosebumps across her skin. Then he trailed kisses down her neck.

Cherie felt something bloom deep inside her chest as Justin led her down the stairs and to the bed. There she slipped off her skirt, then her blouse. His breath came quicker now as he watched. She stepped out of her panties and unhooked her bra, tossing them aside. Justin spread his hands over her breasts, kissed each one, stroked her back, her buttocks, kissed her mouth, her eyes, her shoulders.

Her answer was to peel his T-shirt over his head. She watched as he took off his shorts and underwear, kicking them away, penis hard and erect. If the stars dropped from the heavens to sizzle in the sea at this very moment, she wouldn't care. Everything she wanted and needed was here. He stood still while she explored his smooth, muscular chest with her hands and mouth. Then he pulled the two of them down onto the feather-soft bed, the sound of the boat creaking as they moved in unison. As he kissed her over and over, there seemed such a hunger in him—one that matched her own. Then slowly, deliberately, he loved her body in ways she never knew, and Cherie loved him back. It seemed to her as if the stars doubled and grew brighter in the night sky through the porthole window. When he kissed her mouth yet again, suckled her nipples, and ran his tongue down her stomach, she wanted to stop him, the desire almost painful. He did what he wanted, then spread her legs and tasted her with skill, his tongue warm. She covered her face with her hands and left him to find his way, moaning softly as tears bit at the back of her eyes. As he moved inside her, out, and even deeper, she could hear her heartbeat thundering in her ears. At the last moment, she pushed him off. Surprise crossed his face as she straddled him and loved him back, deliberate, the pleasure immense as every bit of him became hard as steel.

When they finished and lay together, breathless, the waves continued to slosh on the sides of the boat from their lovemaking. Cherie was about to comment on that when she heard a sound and sat up. "Did you hear that?"

Justin jumped out of bed and pulled on his shorts. "Yes. Stay here."

Cherie was already pulling on her clothes. "The shotgun is in the kitchen."

"I'm getting it," said Justin as he left the room.

Cherie followed him out and watched as he retrieved the gun from the corner of the room where he'd left it and pulled back the hammer. He motioned for her to go back in the bedroom, but she shook her head. She pulled open a drawer and took out a flashlight.

When Justin got to the top of the stairs, he stopped and waited. No sound from above. He remained ready; the gun cocked. They stood that way for a time. Cherie crept closer to him, fear filling every nerve in her body. "Turn on the flashlight," he whispered.

Cherie illuminated the top of the stairs. Nothing.

"There's someone up there. I can feel it," she said.

Justin nodded his head imperceptibly. "Let's go up on deck."

They walked on deck, Cherie shining the flashlight around. Still nothing. Could it have been their imaginations? Then a voice from behind them said, "Put the gun down, or I'll shoot her."

16

Justin set the rifle down on the deck and raised his arms.

"Who are you, and what do you want?" said Cherie.

"You're asking a lot of questions for someone with a gun at her back."

Terrified to move, Cherie listened for footsteps, or any other movement on the boat. No other sounds but the night. Whoever their visitor was, he appeared to be alone. "Tell us what you want, and maybe we can work something out," said Cherie, gasping when the man grabbed her shirt from behind and pulled her to him.

"Did Florencio send you?" His arm around her felt sticky with sweat.

"I don't know any Florencio," said Cherie.

"Kick the rifle over here," said the man to Justin, tightening his grip on Cherie. "Now."

Justin did as instructed, giving Cherie a millisecond to act. She lifted her foot and stamped hard on the man's foot, then elbowed him in the stomach. It was enough of a surprise to throw him off-center. She grabbed the arm holding the gun, and the weapon went clattering onto the deck. Justin lunged at the man and tackled him as Cherie retrieved the handgun, which seemed light. She checked the cylinder. Empty.

"His gun wasn't loaded," she told Justin.

Straddling the man, Justin said, "There's some rope up front."

Cherie retrieved the rope, then helped Justin tie the man to a chair.

"Who sent you?" Justin demanded.

The man looked away.

"I'm talking to you." Justin leaned in, his face inches from the man's. "You come onto our boat. You had a reason."

The man didn't speak. Cherie looked at him more closely. He wore ratty shorts and a faded T-shirt and was barefoot, and very thin. His brown hair was overgrown and his beard and mustache could also use a trim. His shirt was dry. "It looks like you didn't come by water. You live on the island, don't you?" said Cherie.

"Untie me, I'll tell you."

"You tell us who you are, then we'll untie you," said Justin.

They waited. The man stayed silent.

"By your accent, you sound American," said Cherie. "How long have you been in Mexico?"

The man gave her a scowl.

"Is Florencio your boss?"

The man looked out into the darkness.

"Does Florencio have something to do with the Americans going missing?" Cherie continued.

This time the man made a slight noise, and his eyes widened.

Cherie stood in front of him, her hands on her hips. "This is what I think. You've been stranded on the island for a while now. Florencio is looking for you. You came on our boat for food. Maybe an escape plan, maybe not. If this

Florencio is as bad as I think he is, you might be better off stranded here."

The man gave her a startled look, then closed down.

"If we were sent by Florencio, we would have contacted him by now," said Cherie. "Tell us what's going on, and we can give you something to eat."

The man considered for a time, then said, "I can't tell you anything until I know who you are."

Cherie paced back and forth in front of him for a moment, then stopped. "You tell me something I can believe, and I'll tell you something. Might even offer it with a bowl of chili."

Justin had seen a lot of interrogations, and they were usually rough and even bloody with a lot of threats and yelling. Cherie's techniques were different. Maybe it was her FBI training, but Justin had a feeling she had mastered the skill, knowing that brute force wasn't always successful.

The man's shoulders slumped forward, and he tried to shift in the chair. "Yes, Florencio is responsible for the missing Americans. Your turn."

Cherie put her hands on her hips again. "Not enough. What is he doing with them?"

The man worked his mouth back and forth as if considering his next words.

Cherie leaned against the railing. "We'd hate to eat without you."

The man considered for several long minutes, then blurted, "It's a ransom scam."

"What do you mean?" asked Cherie.

"They kidnap people, beat up the men, then send their relatives a video of them and demand a ransom payment in cryptocurrency."

"You're saying they. Were you doing this, too?"

"Where's my food?"

"Fair enough," said Cherie, who left to go downstairs.

"What's your name?" Justin asked him when she left.

"Call me Pete," he said, just as Cherie came back with a can of chili and a spoon. The man eyed the food. "That's all you got?"

"You want this, or should I throw it to the fish?" She held the can over the side of the boat.

"No! Don't. I'll eat it."

"Okay, Pete," she said. "Open up."

"You can't untie me?"

"We choose not to. Do you want some food, or not?"

Pete opened his mouth and Cherie spooned some chili in, waiting for him to chew, which he did quickly. He indicated for more chili, then puffed his cheeks with a groan of relief.

She continued feeding him until the can was empty. Then she folded her arms across her chest. "So, tell me, how did you end up on this island?"

"Are you a cop?" His eyes grew large with panic. "And who is he?"

"I have some authority, and I might be able to get you safely off this island, but I'm going to need more information."

The man sighed. "I'm from California. I hooked up with a Mexican woman in LA. It was after my girlfriend kicked me out, and what can I say." He shrugged his shoulders. "Before I know it, I'm knee-deep in cartel business, smuggling stolen cars across the border. They use them to commit crimes, then dump them."

"How long have you been on the island?" said Cherie. "Three weeks."

Cherie could see a genuine look of desperation in Pete's eyes. "What have you been eating? Fish?" she asked.

"When I can catch them, and there's some coconut trees on the island, so I've been drinking the coconut water. I tried eating a berry from this bush but I swelled up something major. Thought I was going to die." He looked around the boat deck. "Is there any more food?"

"We'll see what else we can scrounge up. But first, how'd you get here?"

"I was on a boat with two of Florencio's men and a married couple. They like to get couples, because they can control them by threatening to kill the other one. Florencio also thinks the couples have more money." Pete stopped and a pained expression crossed his face. "One of the men was..." He ran his hand across his face. "Messing with the woman."

"Did he rape her?" asked Cherie.

Pete's eyes were tormented. "The other one was holding the husband back. I tried to stop the man who took advantage of her, but I ended up overboard. It was nighttime. At first, I was going to call out so I could get back onboard, but then I thought, this is my chance to get away. I knew that there are a bunch of small islands out here. I stayed underwater while they shone a light around, then they moved on. I've told you everything. Who do you work for?"

Cherie looked at Justin, then back at Pete. She believed

his story. And he could be useful in leading them to Florencio. "For the FBI."

Pete gave her a stunned look. "I overheard Florencio talking about the FBI."

"What did he say?"

"There's some agent he's got a hard-on for."

"What's the agent's name?"

"Some woman. Her first name was a city or state or something."

"Savannah?"

Pete nodded. "That's it. He's got a big bounty on her head."

"To kill her?"

"No, he wants her alive."

17

Cherie took a few seconds to process the information about Savannah. "What else did you hear?"

Pete's mouth remained closed, but she sensed he knew more.

"A double shot of tequila awaits you. Spill."

"It's clear Florencio has some business with your friend, but you don't ask him any questions, unless you want a bullet through your forehead."

Cherie picked up the computer and headed to the back of the boat to make a call. She dialed Savannah's cell. Voicemail again.

When she returned, Justin gave her a look that said, now what?

"We've got one mystery solved. What they're doing with Americans here. But now we have a lot more questions."

"You want me to start digging for the question you had earlier?" Justin asked her.

Cherie thought about it. Could she justify Justin hacking into the Bureau's website to track Savannah? "Let me think on that."

"You can untie me," said Pete. "I've told you everything, and I won't cause any trouble."

"We need to corroborate your story," said Cherie. "What's your full name, and where did you live before you moved out here?"

"Culver City, and it's Peter Gerard Baker. I was born in Bend, Oregon."

Cherie went to her computer and logged into the Bureau's website, then put his name into the database. "He's not on any wanted lists," she murmured.

"May I?" asked Justin.

Cherie handed over her computer. Justin hacked into the California DMV database and pulled up Pete's driver's license, which had a Culver City address.

"What is your street name and number?" he asked him.

"It's my parents' address. Three-five-three-one Baldwin."

Justin looked at Cherie. "This is your show. You want him untied?"

"If you try anything," she warned Pete, "both of us are trained to kill." She leaned closer to his face. "We won't think twice."

Justin undid the ropes, and Pete remained seated, stretching out his neck. "What I wouldn't give for a shower. Any way I could do that? I'd make it quick."

Cherie also felt dirty, the film of seawater coating her skin sticky and unpleasant. She thought of Savannah and where she might be at that moment, then she turned to Justin. "Go ahead and see what you can find out."

While Justin worked, Cherie sat down and asked Pete, "How did you go from smuggling cars to kidnapping?"

"I had no choice! One night one of Florencio's men didn't show, so he sent me. I was freaked out when I realized we were kidnapping people."

"What do they do with the people after they get the ransom money?"

Pete's brow furrowed. "I haven't seen, but I've heard that they..." He swallowed, then let out a big breath. "That's why I didn't get back on the boat. I was afraid they were going to make me kill people."

"Why did you continue to work for Florencio?"

He ran his hand through his beard. "They threatened my mom and dad. That's what they do."

Cherie nodded.

"I'm hoping they think I drowned," Pete continued, "and are leaving my family alone. My dad has a weak ticker."

"You continue to cooperate, I'll check on them," said Cherie.

Pete looked relieved.

"Mom, Tad needs a new backpack for school. The old one has a hole in it again."

"Then sew it. I showed you how."

"I've sewed it a bunch of times. The material is worn thin. The backpack was cheap."

Her mother had taken off her nursing uniform and stood in her slip and bra. Ever since Patrick's disappearance, she appeared more exhausted and defeated by the day. She got her purse and pulled out a ten-dollar bill. "How much are they? The most I can spare is this. The rent is due tomorrow."

"I think the cheapest one is fifteen," said Cherie. "But I've got some babysitting money."

Cherie's mother's eyes filled with tears. "I should have known Patrick couldn't have made that money working at the yogurt shop. But the car had to be fixed."

"It's not your fault, Mom. Patrick made his own decisions."

Her mother gave Cherie a faint smile. "You've always been a smart girl, ever since you were little. And you're right about your brother. He was always determined. When your father and I bought him a bicycle for his fifth birthday, he stayed in the street until he could ride it without falling. By the time he finally mastered it, he had scraped every visible body part, but he didn't care."

"He's out there somewhere, Mom. He'll come back to us one day."

"You promised me tequila," said Pete after a while.

"I did," said Cherie. She glanced at Justin, at work on the computer. "I'll get the bottle." Below deck, she took the tequila off the kitchen counter, glancing at the bedroom and the tousled covers as she did so. Her mind flashed back to her time with Justin, and a warm glow coursed through her body.

As she grabbed three glasses out of the cupboard, her eye fell on her purse, and she had an idea. She unzipped a side pouch, then pulled out a well-worn photo and slid it into her pocket.

At the sight of the bottle, Pete's eyes lit up. "That's my

favorite brand." He glanced around for the first time. "Is this your boat?"

"We rented it," said Cherie. She set the glasses on the deck. "You want a shot?" she asked Justin.

He shook his head.

She poured one for her and another for Pete, then handed it to him. He took the cup and swallowed the shot all at once. Then he looked out at the water. "It'll be dawn soon. That's how I know how long I've been here. I've been counting the dawns."

They sat that way for a time, watching the water while Justin clicked away on the computer. Before long, the black sky turned gray, then a yellow-white light illuminated the horizon, soon spreading upward and turning the sky a peach color.

"I'm getting closer," Justin said without looking up.

"I've got another question for you," said Cherie, turning to face Pete. She pulled the photo out of her pocket. "Have you seen this man before? This photo is about eleven years old."

Pete leaned forward to study the photo, then he sat back. "No."

"Are you sure?"

"Positive. I never forget a face."

Cherie sighed as she put the photo back in her pocket.

"Who is he?"

"Someone I used to know," said Cherie. "I have reason to believe he's in Mexico."

"Mexico is a big country."

18

As happy as Justin was helping Cherie, he could hear the ticking in the back of his head about his own situation. When things were out of his control, he became nervous as a cat. He had to check in with Billy.

"I'll be right back," he said, then took the computer to the back of the boat to dial his friend's number. After five rings and no answer, he hung up. He chewed the inside of his cheek, trying to figure what his next step would be. Then the VoIP line rang on the computer. It said unknown caller. He clicked answer and waited.

"That you?" It was Billy's voice.

Justin's shoulders relaxed. "Yeah."

"I know they're monitoring my calls, so I got a burner." His tone was hushed. "I'm standing out in the woods right now. I think they bugged the house. I'd play it safe and not use that burner you called me on. They could trace it from my phone."

"How bad was it? Those assholes."

"I've had worse. But I've got some news for you."

"Go on."

"When they thought I was unconscious, I heard Warner talking about your father. It didn't sound good."

Justin's heart rate sped up. "What do you mean?"

"It looks like they're out to get him, too."

"Because of me?" He let out a puff of air.

"They mentioned a woman. Collins was her last name. That ring a bell?"

"Sandra Collins?" Justin would have been happy to never hear that name again.

"Yeah. They only mentioned her name and your old man, and how they wanted you."

Justin's mind began spinning. "I'll make all this up to you."

"I know you will. You still with that woman?"

Justin could hear Pete and Cherie talking at the front of the boat. "Yeah."

"What's her story?"

"That's going to have to wait for later. I gotta go, man." Justin hung up, his heart pounding as he looked out at the early morning sky. No matter what his father had done in the past, he had to find a way to help him.

As Justin carried the laptop to the front of the boat, it pinged. He stopped and checked the screen. "I've got the location," he told Cherie. "She's close."

"As in here in Mexico?"

"Guadalajara."

Pete, who was leaning against the railing, spoke up. "Florencio has a compound in Guadalajara, outside the city." A look of anxiety deepened in the lines of his face.

When Justin told Cherie that Savannah was in Mexico, her worry heightened. She knew her boss could take care of herself in tight situations, but what if she didn't know that Florencio was after her? Cherie knew that anything could go wrong. And it sounded like Savannah was working alone. "How far are we from Guadalajara?" she asked.

"About five hours by car from Puerto Vallarta. What are you thinking?" asked Justin.

Cherie began to pace. "Of going there and trying to find her. Maybe she's in trouble." She stopped. "I can go alone. I know you have other things to figure out."

Pete chimed in. "Hey, how about getting me back to the States?"

"I need you to take me to Florencio's compound first," said Cherie. "That isn't a request. Either you help us out, or you're on your own getting back to the States."

Pete threw up his arms. "Hell no. I'll stay on the island."

"Just get me to the compound. I'll do the rest," said Cherie.

Pete looked from Cherie to Justin. "She's crazy. Tell her."

"You help me with this, I'll be sure to tell my superiors." Cherie persisted. "My boss is high-level in the Bureau. Things will go a lot easier for you. I promise."

Pete slumped into a chair and put his head in his hands while Cherie talked to Justin.

"I'm sorry I haven't been much help with your problem. Did you get through to whoever you were calling?"

Justin motioned with his head to the cabin. When they were inside, he answered her. "It turns out they may also be after my father. And they're using me to get to him. I'm not sure of the details, but there is also a woman involved."

"Who?"

"Billy only heard them mention her name, but I recognized it. She was the reason my parents divorced. My father was having an affair with her."

"What are you going to do?" She tipped her head slightly.

"I'll need to get ahold of my father." He frowned. "He can be a hard man to track down."

"I know how worried you must be," said Cherie. "Once I get out of your way, you'll be able to focus on finding him."

Justin reached out and took Cherie's arm. She looked at him expectantly.

"You sure about going off with Pete? I know he checks out, but he did pull a gun on us."

Cherie was quiet for a moment. "I don't see I have much choice. If Savannah is in danger, I need to find out. And Florencio is holding Americans."

"The photo you showed Pete. Was that your brother?"

Cherie's eyes saddened. "Yes."

"May I see it?"

She pulled it out of her pocket and handed it to him. The young man in the photo looked at the camera with an intense expression. He reminded Justin of Cherie with the same high cheekbones and tentative smile.

"Hey, your computer is making noises," yelled Pete from the deck.

"I'll go," said Cherie.

When she left, Justin took out the burner phone and turned it on, then quickly shot a picture of the photo. As he powered it off, he prayed they hadn't caught the ping.

Cherie returned, and he handed her the photo. "I can see the resemblance," he said.

She smiled and touched her brother's face, then slid the photo back into her pocket. "We better get going."

They went out on deck, and Justin jumped onshore. He untied the boat from the tree and threw the rope onto the deck. As he worked, he glanced at Pete, who stood on deck with an anxious look on his face. He hoped once they were in Puerto Vallarta that Pete wouldn't take off and leave Cherie hanging. Everything in Justin wanted to be with her, to protect her.

"You don't have anything on the island you need to get?" Cherie asked Pete.

"No volleyball that I've been talking to, if that's what you're asking," he said.

Justin laughed, then maneuvered the boat out of the inlet and into open waters. As they headed toward the mainland, he thought about his father and Sandra. When his mother had discovered his father was cheating, she made him pack all his things and leave that very day. The breakup had caused a lasting rift in the family. Justin's father was remarried to another woman today, so why was Sandra's name coming up after all these years?

19

It was midday and the sun hung high in the sky when they approached Puerto Vallarta. Justin slowed the boat and asked Cherie, "Can you drive while I go downstairs and put things away? Just steer us in a straight line. I'll get us to the dock."

Cherie nodded and took over. As she drove and scanned in the distance, she spotted two men on the dock. Picking up the binoculars with one hand, she looked through the lens. They both wore suits and were talking to the man who'd rented them the boat.

"Pete, I need you to drive. I'll be right back."

Pete nodded and took the wheel, a look of intent on his face.

Cherie ran down into the kitchen to find Justin securing the latches.

"Who's steering?" A look of panic crossed his face.

"Pete's steering for a few minutes. I think those men following you are at the dock with the man who rented us the boat."

"Shit," said Justin. "We can't dock there. There are more ports a few miles down. But I don't want them to see me on deck. Just pull the lever to the right of the wheel down, and it'll put the boat into high gear. Head south. I'll take over once we're past the marina."

Cherie nodded and rushed back up the steps and grabbed the wheel. When she shifted the boat into high, water slapped against the sides of the boat, some cascading onboard.

"I need you to keep a lookout," cried Cherie to Pete over the boat's engine. "Let me know if you see anyone coming after us."

The catamaran suddenly thudded on a wave, jolting Cherie. She grabbed the steering wheel even harder and focused on getting as far away as possible. After she had driven for a while, Justin poked his head up and yelled, "Anyone following us?"

"No!" Pete shouted back.

Justin came to stand beside Cherie.

"Can I slow down now?" she asked.

He took over the wheel but kept up the pace. "I checked. There's a dock further down the coast. You and Pete keep a lookout. We should be there soon."

A few minutes later, they came to a small cove with a few slips. Justin slowed the boat, then entered. No one was about except for an older man tending to a small fishing boat.

"*Hola, Señor*," Justin called out. "We need to park. *Estacionarse.*"

The man eyed the boat, then gestured to the farthermost slot. Justin drove over to the slip, then jumped out and secured the boat.

The man approached, his gait slow. He wore a Panama hat, and his skin was weathered brown from days spent on the water. He stopped to peer up at them, his eyes wary. "*Yo conozco esa barco. Mi primo se encarga de eso*," he said to Justin.

"What did he say?" asked Cherie.

"He says his cousin takes care of this boat."

Justin spoke more with the man, then turned to Cherie. "I'm pretty much cleaned out after paying to rent the boat and for the bribe. Do you have any money? He's going to return the boat to his cousin. I told him we ran out of fuel and have to catch a flight."

Cherie paid the man, then they disembarked quickly. After they had walked for a time away from the dock, she asked Justin, "What are we going to do now?"

Justin stopped to face her. "Do you trust your boss?"

"Yes, with my life."

"No chance she'd be somehow caught up in the cartel here?"

"No, never."

"I'm going with you to find her."

"But what about your father?"

"As long as I outrun the boys in black, my problem can wait. I can't—" Justin put his hands on her shoulders. "I wouldn't forgive myself if something happened to you."

Cherie felt tension she didn't know she had been holding subside. "Are you sure? I've got Pete to help me. Wait." She glanced around. "Where is he?"

"Shh," Justin warned, then guided her to turn and continue walking. "Florencio's men could have tracked him, or he ran. Either way, we don't want to attract attention," he said in a low voice. "Let's go to that bodega over there."

When they got to the bodega, full of families having a midday meal, Justin led them to a corner table facing the entrance.

"*Un plato de tacos*," he said when a waitress approached and set glasses of water in front of them.

She looked at Cherie, who said, "The same."

When the waitress left, Justin said, "Let's get our bearings here for a few minutes, then catch a ride to Guadalajara. If we leave in the next hour, we'll get there by nightfall."

"We need a gun," said Cherie in a low voice.

"I've got one."

"How'd you pull that off?" she asked, surprised.

"When I went down to put things away, including the rifle, I found a handgun further back in that cupboard. A bit of luck for us. I probably shouldn't have taken it, but us going into Florencio's camp unarmed seems like suicide."

"It may be suicide anyway," said Cherie. "What if Pete was scamming us all along, or if they did nab him and he tells them we're coming?"

"That's a chance we're going to have to take."

"Can you see if Savannah's cellphone is still pinging there?"

Justin got out the laptop and pulled up a screen as the waitress set down two plates of tacos and a bowl of salsa.

"*Gracias,*" said Cherie. "Do you speak English?"

The woman nodded.

"We're looking for someone to give us a ride to Guadalajara. Do you know anyone?"

"*Sí,* my nephew, Pedro."

"Is he available today?"

"I go call him."

"One other thing," said Cherie, pulling her suitcase out from under the table. "Would you happen to know if I could trade this for a backpack? It's a good case, but it's too bulky for my travels."

The waitress eyed the case and nodded.

When she left, Cherie asked, "What'd you find out?"

Justin shut the computer. "Your boss's cellphone hasn't budged since I accessed it yesterday."

20

"Staying put doesn't sound like Savannah," said Cherie.

"I know what you're thinking. But there are a million reasons why her phone could be stationary, including that she lost it. And before you tell me she doesn't lose things, everyone does."

Cherie spooned some salsa onto a taco. "You're right. We don't know what we're dealing with until we get there."

They ate in silence for a time, the sound of diners and drinkers creating a wall of noise around them. She willed herself not to worry about Savannah. Her boss was the most resourceful person she knew.

The waitress approached then with a young man by her side. He had black, wavy hair and wore board shorts and a T-shirt that said Led Zeppelin. "This is Pedro. He can drive you to Guadalajara."

Pedro smiled and jutted out his hand to Justin. *"Mucho gusto."*

"Nice to meet you, as well," said Justin.

Then Pedro turned to Cherie and shook her hand. "We can go to Guadalajara when you are ready, *Señorita.*"

The waitress handed Cherie a backpack. She quickly unzipped her suitcase and began transferring the contents to the backpack. Once she finished stuffing it all in, she said, "No time like the present."

A few minutes later, they were situated in the back of Pedro's battered Honda Civic. The young man looked at them in the rearview mirror. "It will take five hours to get to Guadalajara." Then he pulled away from the curb and headed into traffic, tapping his horn as they traveled in and out between cars. When they passed by a fruit and vegetable stand and the young man stocking the shelves with melons saw them, he gave them a hearty wave.

"My brother," said Pedro proudly.

Cherie woke up to the sound of her mother's voice. She glanced at the clock. Just past six in the morning. Too early for school. Tad still slept soundly. She slid out of bed and walked softly to the bedroom door, cracked it open and listened.

"Thanks, Dad, I didn't know what else to do. I know funds are tight for you and Mom right now. I'll pay you back. The private eye says he will find him, if he's still..." Cherie's heart clutched when she heard her mother choke back a sob. "Thanks. I know. I won't give up hope."

Cherie heard her mother pouring coffee, then she spoke again. "The kids are doing okay. Tad doesn't understand what is going on, but Cherie is another story. She and

Patrick were so close. They were there for each other when I couldn't be after Paul died."

More silence, then Cherie's mother spoke. "Thanks, Pop. Tell Mom I love her."

Cherie heard the receiver click, then her mother's soft sobs. She was about to go back to bed, but instead she softly shut the door behind her and went to the kitchen. Her mother looked at her, startled, then turned her head and brushed the tears away.

"You're up early." She took a sip of coffee.

"I heard you on the phone. Was that grandpa?"

"Yes."

"He's giving you money for a private investigator to look for Patrick?"

"You were eavesdropping?"

"Do you really think we can find him?"

Her mother sat down at the kitchen island and indicated for Cherie to come sit beside her.

"I'm going to do my best to find your brother. This investigator came highly recommended. The police have given up. But he's not just another missing person to us." She put her hand on Cherie's. "And he never, ever will be."

Cherie looked down at her mother's hand encasing hers and felt the ache in her chest she'd come to live with. "I miss him so much, Mom."

During the long drive on the dusty highway, Cherie found herself nodding off. It was hot in the car, though Pedro ran the air conditioning. At one point, she awoke and pushed her hair back, then looked over at Justin. "How long was I sleeping?"

"A couple of hours," he said. "You were talking."

"What did I say?"

"Savannah's name. And then your brother's."

Cherie sighed. "I just don't think I could take it if someone else I care about disappears."

At Cherie's words, Justin reached over and pulled her to him. As she nestled her head against his chest, he said, "We'll find her."

"Then I'll help you," she said. "I promise."

Justin kissed the top of her head. "I know you will."

Justin had been with many women. But it wasn't until that moment that he realized he hadn't really known any of them. And he certainly hadn't cared for them like he cared for Cherie. He wasn't sure how this thing was going to shake out, but the only future he could see for himself was one with Cherie in it.

21

They pulled into Guadalajara at sunset as the lights in the city began to blink on. Cherie yawned and stretched her body, loosening the kinks from dozing.

"Where are you going in the city?" asked Pedro as he drove onto a crowded street brimming with cars, mopeds, and pedestrians.

"Drop us off at the Radisson in the center of town. You know it?" said Justin.

"Oh, *sí, sí*, that is a nice place," he said and smiled. "You have a good time there, no?"

After maneuvering through rush hour traffic, he pulled up in front of the hotel. Cherie handed him two large bills. "Will this cover things, Pedro?"

He glanced at the money and nodded. "*Gracias, Señorita.*"

When Pedro had driven away, Cherie turned to Justin. "So, we check in and use this as a home base and figure out next steps?"

"If you have enough cash left."

"I think I do, but it won't last much longer."

They made their way to the front desk where an older

gentleman stood at attention. "*Señor y Señorita*, do you have a reservation?"

"No, we don't. Do you have any vacancies?" asked Justin.

The man checked the computer. "We have a room on the sixth floor. Will that do?"

"Yes," said Justin. "I'm hoping we can pay cash. Our wallets were stolen."

"*Ay, no, pobrecitos*," said the man. "I think we can make an exception. If you don't mind paying ahead in cash. And we'll need extra for collateral." He gave them an expectant look.

Cherie pulled out some bills. "I think this will cover two or three nights."

The man nodded in approval and handed them two keycards. "The elevator is across the way, past the restaurant."

As they walked away, Justin said in a low voice, "You gotta love Mexico's payoff system. That would have never happened in the States."

Cherie hit the up arrow for the elevator. "The best part is no paper trail."

When they got into the room, furnished in a tropical theme, complete with a lime and cream duvet covered in palm trees, Cherie stood next to the air-conditioner and made a hum of appreciation as the cool air hit her skin. "This feels so good after that hot, sticky car."

Justin pulled open a small refrigerator in the room's kitchenette. "Want a water?"

"Yes, definitely."

He pulled out two bottles and handed her one.

"How about we check out the compound on Google maps, then go scout it," Cherie said.

Justin threw his empty bottle in a nearby trashcan. "How about a shower first to clean up and clear our heads."

"Good idea," said Cherie. "Did you want to go first?"

JULIE BAWDEN DAVIS

Justin chuckled. He didn't speak as he walked over and turned her around, then pulled her V-neck top up and over her head. He helped as she shimmied out of her skirt, then directed her to a nearby chair. When she was sitting, he took her left sandal off, massaging her foot, kissing the instep, then did the right foot.

At the look of intensity on Justin's face, Cherie felt a heated desire come over her. It was apparent sex was something he enjoyed.

"I can't not touch you," he said, pulling her up and to him. He trailed his tongue along her neck. "You're very sweaty," he murmured as she felt her body yield to him. Then he led her to the bathroom, where he turned the shower on. She watched as he took off his shirt and shorts until he stood before her all-rippled muscles, his arousal clear. He kissed her again, this time deep and demanding as he pressed himself against her. When they pulled apart, he undid her bra and pushed her panties down. She kicked them aside, then stepped into the shower and stood beneath the water, letting its steamy, wet heat run over her head and body. Justin got in after her. Seeing him naked and wet flamed the passion already inside her. He raised her arms over her head and pressed her body against the shower wall, running his tongue between her breasts and down to her belly button, making her laugh and gasp almost at the same time. Then he turned her around and leaned her over, the water coursing along her back. She planted her hands against the shower tile as he kissed her shoulders, then took hold of her hips and spread her legs to thrust slowly inside her. As he possessed her, Cherie felt like begging him never to stop. Then his hands tightened on her hips and he came with a final trembled jerk. They stayed that way for a few moments as Justin caught his breath, then he turned her around and soaped her breasts, dropping on his knees, water flowing over him, as he used the tip of his tongue to bring her to orgasm. When he finished, she heard him say something. It sounded like I love you. Did she imagine what he said? Should she ask him? Reply? She leaned against the wall in the corner of the shower, spent, watching as he lathered up, rinsed and got out, then grabbed a towel.

"I'll be out in a minute," she said. "I'm going to wash my hair."

"Okay," he said, and went into the next room, but not before leaning in to kiss her on the mouth.

Justin toweled off and went out into the room, closing the bathroom door behind him. He hadn't meant to tell Cherie he loved her. It had just slipped out. When she didn't reply, he took that as a sign he had gone too far. She hadn't said anything to him that would indicate she felt that deeply. Had his desire for her been too much? He pulled on his shorts and sat down at the table, opened the laptop and got to work.

When Cherie came out a few minutes later, their eyes locked for a moment. Then she looked away and cleared her throat. "What did you find out about the compound?"

"It looks tight, as we figured. It's a little ways out of town to the north. I'm trying to tap into their security system, so we can see what's going on there."

"You can do that? I am officially impressed."

Justin kept typing. "This is why my superiors refer to me as an asset."

Cherie sat down across from Justin. "The terminology sounds almost..." She trailed off.

Justin looked up and met her eyes. "Inhuman?"

She nodded.

"It's both a curse and a blessing." He stopped typing and cracked his knuckles. "At first, it makes you feel special, but then you begin to feel used. And when you realize that no one really cares about you, that they only care about what you can do for them, and they'll protect what you can do at all costs, even if it harms you, it's sobering. Then one day, you become a liability. And we both know what they do with liabilities."

Just then, the computer pinged, and he checked the screen. "We're in!"

"Inside the compound?"

"Come take a look."

Cherie pulled her chair to the other side of the table next to Justin. "It's a big place. Is that the security room?" she asked when he flipped to a screen showing two men overseeing computer screens.

"Yeah, and they have no idea we're watching them. You've got to love the irony."

Justin tapped some keys, and they were in a garage filled with cars. "Looks like his fleet." More taps and they came to a massive kitchen, where an older woman was making a cup of tea. Then several empty hallways. Next, an indoor pool. The room was empty, the water still.

Justin was thinking that maybe they weren't going to find anything when they came to a wing of the house with much more activity. Several men talking in one room, then another room with guards standing outside. He checked a small room, and Cherie gasped. There, tied to a chair, was a blonde woman. Her head was slumped forward. Next to her was a man also tied to a chair.

"That's Savannah!" said Cherie.

"And that's Pete," said Justin.

22

"Why is Pete with Savannah?"

"They must think there's a connection," said Justin.

Cherie put her head in her hands. "This just makes no sense. I work closely with Savannah. Why would I have not known about this?"

Justin sighed. "You'd be surprised what people keep from you."

Cherie stopped. "I'm sorry. That was insensitive. Did you dig up anything else about your father?"

"Not much. I need to talk to him somehow without being detected. To warn him."

"Well, if we can get Savannah out of this mess, I'm sure she can arrange that. We need to get to the compound."

"What we need is to stop for a beat, or else we'll be useless," said Justin. "Let's get a few hours of sleep."

Cherie pulled some clean clothes out of her bag. "Savannah is in trouble. I'm not staying here wasting time. I'll go by myself."

Justin reached out and took Cherie by the arms. "We're not going to do Savannah any good if we go in and become hostages, too. Let's rest three or four hours. We'll go to the compound while it's still dark."

Cherie knew what Justin said made sense. And despite the adrenaline driving her from being worried about Savannah, she was exhausted.

"You sound like Savannah right now," she said.

"Four hours tops." Justin took Cherie's hand and led her to the bed. He pulled down the covers, and they both slid under the cool sheets. "This does feel good," she said, stretching out on the soft mattress.

Justin punched up his pillow beside her, then settled down, his arm touching hers. "Uh, huh," he murmured.

As they lay there, the air-conditioner humming, Cherie thought how good it felt to be here with Justin, regardless of all the turmoil. She recalled their time in the shower. Did he tell her he loved her? And if so, did he mean it? She lay there drumming up the courage to ask him, then finally turned on her side to do so. "Justin?" she whispered. But he was asleep.

It was still night when Justin shook Cherie awake. She opened her eyes to see that he had dressed, and the room smelled of coffee.

"As promised, four hours," he said.

Cherie yawned. "Give me a second. Can you pour me some coffee?"

Justin filled a cup and handed it to her. "I did some recon

while you were sleeping. Come look at this." He gestured toward the computer screen. "It's likely that the nightshift guards are going to change soon. Say around 5 or 6 am. It's 3:30 now. That gives us time to get there and position ourselves. We can storm our way in when the exchange occurs."

"That's pretty risky," said Cherie, getting up to stand beside him. "Looks like they've got at least four guards on duty."

"I don't see any other way to get in as quickly as we want to. This will take them off guard. I'm sure no one messes with Florencio's compound. If there was a rival gang coming in, they'd already know and be on high alert waiting for them."

"Let me check something first," said Cherie. "I want to see if Jasmine in the lab sent me anything."

Cherie logged onto her email and began scrolling. "This is odd."

"What's that?"

"I emailed Jasmine to see if she'd heard anything about Savannah. There's an automatic message saying she is off on an extended leave."

"That is suspicious," said Justin.

Cherie took a sip of coffee and reached for a sugar packet. As she opened it, she said, "I keep wracking my brain for anything that would hint at any of this. The last I heard, Savannah was working an identity theft case."

"Maybe they're related," said Justin.

"How so?"

He pointed to the computer. "May I?"

Cherie handed it over and he began typing. "There was something I saw when I was unearthing stones surrounding Florencio. Some charges that were dropped against him here in Mexico." He stopped and scanned the screen. "He was brought in last year on racketeering and forgery charges. The forgeries involved passports."

"So, they could be taking the passports of the Americans they're killing and using them to make forged ones," said Cherie.

"Exactly." He closed the computer. "You ready?"

Cherie took a final slug of coffee and stood. Then she emptied her backpack of the clothing, leaving the gun inside, and zipped it up.

They walked through the hushed hallway, neither speaking. Instead of taking the elevator, Justin pointed to the stairway. Quickly, they descended, then made their way through the hotel lobby, passing by the nighttime clerk absorbed in a book at the front desk.

"We're going to need to catch a taxi," said Justin as he pushed open the lobby doors.

It was still dark outside and the air hung heavy with humidity. A lone taxi sat near the entrance. When the driver saw them, he called out, "You need ride?"

They got in the cab, and Justin gave the driver Florencio's address. When he did so, the man's eyes widened. "This wrong address, no?" he asked in stilted English.

Cherie handed him some bills. "It's the right address."

The man swallowed and looked like he might refuse, then turned around and put the car in gear. As he headed onto the street, he glanced back in the rearview mirror, a look of concern in his dark eyes. After a few minutes, he said, "I drop you off a block away."

As they drove, Cherie felt her stomach tight with nerves. This always happened when she was on an operation, but usually Savannah was sitting beside her. She glanced at Justin; his expression was tense. They were rounding a corner when headlights flashed behind them. Cherie looked to see a black sedan approaching quickly.

"*Ay, no,*" said the driver. "What I do?"

"Keep driving," ordered Justin.

"I no want trouble. I have wife and children," the man cried as the sedan pulled up next to them, the headlights continuing to flash on and off.

Cherie braced to duck if shots fired, but instead the sedan's back window lowered and a man shouted, "This is the United States National Security Agency. We have permission from the Mexican government to pull you over."

The driver immediately steered to the side of the street and braked.

"Dammit," said Justin.

Within seconds, a man advanced on the car and flashed an ID, announcing, "Justin Kincaid, you are being apprehended for going AWOL from the United States Marines."

23

As they pulled Justin from the car, Cherie tried to meet his eyes, but they quickly turned him away and cuffed him. Within seconds, they shoved him in the back of the sedan, then slammed the door and sped off.

"*Señorita*, where you want to go?" asked the driver, his eyes wide. She could see his hands trembling on the steering wheel.

"Take me back to the hotel."

The man looked relieved and put the car in gear.

"I'm sorry for all the trouble," she said when they got back to the hotel.

"No problem," he said. "I hope you okay, lady."

Cherie got out of the car and trudged through the lobby. When she got to their room, she sat on the edge of the bed where the covers were thrown back from when she and Justin had napped together. She took several deep breaths, gripping the side of the bed, trying to still the panic, but before long, a familiar feeling of abandonment overtook her. She put her head in her hands and began weeping.

A few minutes later, she got up and dabbed her face with

tissue, then shook her head. Enough with your pity party, Cherie, she said to herself. Time to figure out a plan B for getting Savannah out. She sat down at the table and pulled open her laptop.

"Are these cuffs really necessary?" asked Justin.

Warner turned to him. "You were a tough man to track down, Kincaid."

"How did you find me? The burner phone?"

The man raised his eyebrows. "I was surprised you turned it on. A rookie move for someone with your expertise. It must have been important." Warner eyed him, as if waiting for Justin to comment, but he wouldn't give him the satisfaction.

Warner turned back around in his seat as they waited at a gate. A guard approached to open it.

"You're taking me to the American Embassy?" asked Justin.

"For now. While we wrap a few things up."

Justin thought about Cherie as they drove up the long drive to the low-slung building framed by giant palm trees. He hoped she wouldn't go to Florencio's compound on her own, but from what he'd come to know about her over the last few days, including her fierce loyalty, he knew she would try. And there was nothing he could do to save her.

While Cherie surveyed Florencio's compound, she thought of who she could contact about Savannah. Technically, she should call this in, but the person she'd normally call things into was Savannah. And now Jasmine was MIA. There had been talk recently about a mole at the agency. Was a mole responsible for Savannah now being in the clutches of a cartel boss?

Cherie then saw something that gave her an idea. Two women entered the compound with cleaning supplies. She checked the camera overlooking the street and found their vehicle, a van with the words *Limpieza de Hidalgo Servicio*. Putting the name into the search engine, she waited while an address came up. The offices were within walking distance. She checked the time. Nearly five am. She'd wait until six, then go apply for a cleaning job.

The day had dawned clear and warm when Cherie made her way to the cleaning service office. A bell clanged when she opened the front door and stepped inside to find a bald man pouring a large tub of green fluid into individual bottles. Pine scent filled the air.

"*Si, Señorita*, can I help you?" The man turned to her. "You need your home cleaned?"

"Actually, I'm looking for a job," she said. "This is embarrassing, but all my money and credit cards were stolen." She held up empty hands. "I need to earn bus fare back to San Diego. My family won't send me any money. They say it serves me right to have been robbed."

The man stared at Cherie for a moment, his brows knitted, as if trying to digest what she just told him. Finally, he asked, "You want to be a cleaner for money?"

Cherie nodded. "I actually clean houses back home, so this would be perfect."

The man kept staring.

"I'm a very good worker," she assured him. "And I'm willing to work for your lowest pay."

At the mention of cheap labor, the man perked up. He set down the tub. "We have a factory that needs cleaning. I'll be right back."

When he left the room, Cherie ran to the wall and checked out the schedule hanging on a clipboard. She scanned the sheet, locating a column that said Flor. Sure enough, two maids scheduled for early that morning. It looked like two more would be going in for the three pm to nine pm shift. She heard footsteps in the hallway and ran back to where he had left her.

"I think this will fit you." He handed her a uniform. "You can change in the bathroom."

"I'm sorry, I can't start work until this afternoon. But I can work the night, if needed."

Hidalgo rubbed the nub of beard at the tip of his chin, then went to check the schedule. "We could use someone to work nights. Come back at 2:30. What is your name?"

"Olivia. Thank you, *Señor Hidalgo.*"

The man smiled and went back to pouring cleaning fluid.

Out in the street, Cherie let out a big sigh. As she walked back to the hotel, she thought through her plan. They would likely have metal detectors, and at the very least search all who entered. There was no way she could enter with a gun.

The call came when Cherie was working late in the lab

one night her second year at the Bureau. She glanced at the screen, *caller unknown*. She set down the test-tube she was holding and pulled off her gloves, then picked up her cellphone and tentatively said, "Hello?"

"Sis, it's me," said her brother on the other end of the line. "I can't talk long. I just wanted you to know I'm okay."

Cherie stood up so fast, her stool clattered to the floor. "Patrick, where are you?"

"I can't tell you. I just wanted to say I love you. I'm sorry about all of this."

"Mom will be happy to hear you're okay," said Cherie, steadying herself against the counter.

"You can't tell her," he said.

"Why?"

"If they try to question her or Tad, they would say something. I know you won't."

"But Patrick," said Cherie, feeling her brother slipping away. "Just tell me where you are. I'll come to you."

"I can only say it's warm where I am, and I'm safe. I get to eat my favorite food every day. I have to go now, Sis. I'm not sure when I'll be able to call again. Give Mom and Tad a hug for me."

As Cherie stood there with the phone in her hand, staring through a blur of tears at the empty screen, she thought about Patrick's favorite food—Mexican.

24

Cherie left a little after two o'clock wearing the maid's outfit. When she arrived at the office, Hidalgo greeted her. "There you are. We have a van to take you to the residence. This is Flora. She speaks English and will tell you what to do."

A short, young woman wearing a uniform like Cherie, her black hair in a ponytail, jumped out of a chair. "Nice to meet you."

"Nice to meet you, too, Flora," she said. "Your English is very good."

Flora looked pleased. "I studied in the United States for two months."

Hidalgo clapped his hands. "It's time to go. The van is out front." His eyes went to the pocket of Cherie's uniform. "This client requires that you go in without a cellphone. Is that one in your pocket?"

Cherie knew she wouldn't be able to lie her way out of this. "Yes, but what do I do with it?"

Hidalgo held out his hand. "I will hold it for you."

Cherie didn't want to give Hidalgo her phone, but it

appeared to be a deal breaker. She reluctantly traded it for a bucket of cleaning supplies.

"Have you been to the place we're going to clean before?" asked Cherie as they headed away in a van.

Flora, who had been smiling until then, frowned. "Yes." She hesitated. "The owner is a powerful man. It is important you do just what I say. He is—how you say in English—picky."

"I'll follow your lead," Cherie said.

When they arrived at the compound, the wrought iron gates opened immediately. Then the van clipped past immaculate green lawns dotted with iron statuary. Beyond the sprawling mansion, she saw a tennis court.

"Wow," said Cherie. "This place is big. We don't need to clean it all tonight, I hope."

Flora laughed. "Only part of it, and sometimes they have us help the kitchen staff with cleanup when they have a lot of guests."

The van dropped them at the back of the mansion, where they entered through a servant's entrance. As soon as they walked in, a large Mexican woman wearing an apron began spouting orders at Flora. Then she looked at Cherie with a critical eye. "*Quién es ella?*"

Flora answered in Spanish, then said in a low voice to Cherie. "She asked who you are, and I told her you're new. We need to wait for a guard to come check you."

Cherie acted surprised. "Check me? For what?"

Flora reddened. "Weapons and drugs. It is much different here in Mexico."

When the guard, a large man over six feet, hairy forearms covered in tattoos, finally came, he patted Cherie down quickly, then checked their buckets of cleaning supplies. Once done, he nodded an okay and lumbered away.

"Come with me," said Flora. Cherie followed, observing as they walked. The hum of activity confirmed what she'd seen on the surveillance footage—the place was much more than a residence. They finally arrived at a row of bedrooms that looked like a guest wing. Cherie pictured the layout she'd seen online and determined that Savannah was being held down the hall she now stood in and to the left.

"Clean the bathroom first," said Flora. "I'll be in the next room."

Cherie went into a bedroom, bigger than her apartment back in DC, and glanced around. Then she went into the bathroom and shut the door. Standing there for a moment to get her bearings, she took a deep breath. *You're in,* she whispered to herself. *Now you just need to get to Savannah.* Part of her wanted to run down the hallway and bang on doors, but she knew she had to be smarter than that. She had six hours to figure out how to get Savannah out of here.

They put Justin in a small room without windows, and he'd been here for several hours. He drummed his fingers on the arms of the chair where he sat, his thoughts once again going to Cherie.

Just then the door opened and in walked a woman. She wore a black, tailored suit and had her platinum blond hair pulled back in a tight bun. "Hello, Justin," she said, stopping just inside the doorway. "I'm not sure if you remember me."

Justin remained seated. "I would never forget the woman who broke up my parents' marriage," he said. "I would ask how you're doing, Sandra, but it's obviously better than me. You work for the NSA now?"

Sandra closed the door behind her and came over to the table where Justin sat, pointing to a chair across from him. "May I?"

Justin didn't respond.

Sandra pulled out the chair and sat down across from him, setting a cellphone on the table. "Yes, I am Director of Terrorism Intel for the NSA. It's unfortunate that things came to this. I would have liked to meet on better terms."

Justin snorted. "What is it that this has come to? Tell me. I've done nothing wrong."

Sandra crossed her arms and sat back in her chair. "I know that."

Justin sat up and leaned toward her. "Then what am I doing here?"

"You don't know why?"

Justin threw up his hands. "Enlighten me. Is it my father? Are you trying to get to him through me? Is the Sudan coverup I stepped into the NSA's mess?"

Justin waited while Sandra continued to study him. "You really don't know. I'd thought with all your skills that you would have..." She trailed off.

"Clearly, I missed something," said Justin.

"This involves your mother."

Justin was shocked. "What does she have to do with any of this?"

"We believe your mother is married to a terrorist."

Justin laughed. "Miles? You've got to be kidding me. He's a carpet salesman. This is crazy."

"We have solid evidence. The only question is whether your mother is complicit."

Justin leaned back and frowned. Sandra was serious. "I thought Miles was American."

"He has dual citizenship. Syria."

"Well, I can guarantee my mother doesn't know. And where does my father fit into this?"

"Your father is being questioned in DC."

Justin put his head in his hands, then looked back up at Sandra. "This has nothing to do with what I uncovered in Sudan?"

"That is an ongoing investigation, but your name has been cleared. Is that why you ran?"

"I thought I was being framed." Justin wrapped his knuckles on the table. "There's money in my account that I didn't put there. I'm sure you've seen it."

"We've traced the money back to one of your stepfather's accounts. It looks like he was suspecting we were onto him, so he started diverting funds."

"Look, there's something I need to take care of," said Justin. "You want me to take a polygraph test, I will. You probably know that since what happened with you and my father, our family isn't close. As a matter of fact, I rarely see my mother."

"We've ascertained that, but we needed to be sure," said Sandra.

"So, this is a formality?" said Justin, his anger rising. "You've already got my mother in custody, haven't you?"

Sandra glanced at the clock on the wall. "The FBI is currently raiding your stepfather's carpeting warehouse in Los Angeles. We expect to find bombmaking activity. And your mother is being picked up at her home in Bel Air as we speak."

"Bel Air?" Justin said. "The last I knew she lived in Sherman Oaks."

Sandra nodded. "Your mother had to have wondered how her carpeting salesman husband could afford a home in one of the toniest areas of Los Angeles."

"I have to get out of here," said Justin, standing up. "Just give me a few hours."

The cellphone on the table rang then. Sandra picked it up. "This call will let me know if you're free to go."

25

Cherie searched the contents of the bathroom, looking for anything she might use for a weapon. Sliding a slim drawer open under the vanity, she found a rattail metal comb. Bingo. Just then Flora knocked on the door. "How's it going in there?" she called.

Cherie stuffed the comb into her pocket, then flushed the toilet and opened the door with the toilet bowl cleaner in her hand. "Great."

Flora's eyes swept the bathroom. "They like us to keep the doors open here."

"Oh, okay. Sorry."

"Make sure to bleach the toilet."

Cherie nodded. "I usually do that last."

"When you're done with this room, hurry and change the sheets. They have guests coming in."

"I'll speed it up," said Cherie, turning to extract the bleach bottle from the pail.

When Flora had gone, Cherie eyed the bottle. That would make another good weapon. She loosened the lid and carefully put it back in the pail.

Justin raced through the streets of Guadalajara toward the hotel. They had finally let him out with instructions to return to the US as soon as possible to report to his Master Sergeant. When he arrived at the hotel, he went up to the front desk, glad to see the same man who had checked them in. "I seem to have lost my keycard," he said. "I can't get ahold of my wife."

The man looked at him over the top of his bifocals. "I will give you another key, *Señor*. How is your stay? Will you be checking out in the morning?"

"I think so, but I'll give you more cash, if not," he said. The man nodded and handed him the keycard.

Justin walked quickly to the staircase, taking three steps at a time to the sixth floor. As he ran down the hallway, he prayed that he'd find Cherie. But the room was empty.

"Where are you?" he said out loud. Glancing around, he spotted the backpack on the bed. He went to open it and found the gun inside. Suddenly, he felt hopeful. Maybe she hadn't gone to try to extract Savannah after all.

He checked the rest of her things, noticing that the only thing missing was her cellphone. He turned his phone on, then dialed her number. It rang several times before going to voicemail. Justin dialed it again. A man's voice answered this time. *"Es esto una emergencia?"*

"Who's this?" asked Justin.

"I am Hidalgo. Olivia is out cleaning for a client. Who is this?"

"Her husband," said Justin. "When will she be finished?"

"At nine."

Justin hung up the phone. So, Cherie had gotten herself into Florencio's compound as a cleaner. He dialed Billy's number.

"I thought you weren't using this phone?" said Billy by way of greeting.

"We're okay with the NSA. I'll explain later. Right now, I've got a situation. I need some manpower."

"Where are you?" asked Billy.

"Guadalajara."

"I'm about an hour away. Tell me what you need."

Cherie hurried through the cleaning of each room, her mind spinning, knowing Savannah was nearby. When she was putting the finishing touches on a bed, she heard Flora's and a man's voice in the hallway. She went to the doorway to see the maid pinned against the wall by a guard.

"Stop it, Roberto. I need to get back to work," said Flora, her voice bordering on pleading.

"Hey, what's up?" asked Cherie.

Flora took the opportunity to step away from him. "Roberto was just leaving."

The guard turned and looked Cherie up and down. "I haven't seen you before, *chica*."

"Leave her alone," said Flora. "She's visiting from America."

"*Una Americana*. I like that." He sauntered over to Cherie.

"I'll handle this, Flora," Cherie said over his shoulder. "Just go clean a room."

Flora looked hesitant, then turned and left.

"Isn't she a little young for you?" Cherie asked the guard after Flora was out of earshot.

He shrugged one shoulder. "Maybe."

Cherie moved in closer. "I'd think a man like you would want a woman." She quickly ran her eyes down his body, then gave him her most seductive smile.

A surprised grin covered his face. "You that woman?"

Cherie was just inches from him. "I could be. First, I want you to do something for me."

Roberto jutted out his chin. "Yeah, *hermosa*, what is that?"

"I know whose house this is. I want a tour."

"*Hijole*, you don't ask much."

"Give me a quick tour, and I promise you won't be disappointed."

Roberto shook his head. "I can't do that."

Cherie backed up. "It could have been fun, but okay. I've got work to do." She turned to go back into a room when he called after her.

"Okay. Then you're going to do whatever I say."

Cherie turned around slowly. "If anyone stops us, you can say I got lost and you were showing me the way," she said.

"There isn't much to see," he said as they walked. "Just a bunch of rooms." When they came to the hallway that led to where Savannah was being held, the guard turned to go back.

"What about down there?" said Cherie, pointing. "I want to see everything."

"We can't go there."

"You don't show me everything, I don't show you anything." She gave him a coy smile.

"Shit, okay, but we need to make it quick."

As they headed down the hallway, Cherie's blood pressure ramped up. She could tell Roberto was nervous himself. When they came to a set of double doors where another guard stood, the man did a doubletake and exclaimed, "*Que estas haciendo?*"

"Just giving the lady a tour. Then she's going to give me a tour."

"*Mierda, hombre*, you know how stupid you are? If the boss catches you, you're dead."

Now was her only shot, thought Cherie, who grabbed the bleach and flung the liquid at Roberto's eyes. He began screaming, and she pulled out the metal comb and lunged at the guard in front of the door, ramming it into his abdomen. As he grabbed his stomach and doubled over, she pushed open the doors and ran down the hallway. She yanked the doors open to several rooms. All empty. Then she came to the last room and pulled it open, stopping herself from crying out at what she saw.

26

There slouched over in a chair in the center of the room was Savannah. Cherie raced over and knelt in front of her.

"Savannah," she whispered, gently shaking her by the arms. When she didn't respond, Cherie felt her wrist. There was a pulse. Working quickly, she untied her hands and was freeing her legs when she heard a movement behind her. Cherie stood and swung around. There, flanked by two guards, stood a man with a pockmarked face and a dark expression in his eyes. He held an unlit cigar in one hand.

"Miss Tomlinson, while I'm impressed at your ingenuity, you are a fool to penetrate my fortress."

"You're Florencio," said Cherie. "It was your men who tried to grab me at the airport."

He examined the end of the cigar. "It's surprising to me that with your wit and intelligence you would waste your talents at the FBI." He pulled a lighter out of his pocket. "Now I have a quandary. What to do with two FBI agents."

Cherie glanced back at Savannah, then at Florencio. "What do you want with her?"

He put the cigar between his teeth and lit it, taking several puffs that he blew her way. "Information."

"I'm sure we can work something out," said Cherie, panic in her throat. "An agreement we can all be satisfied with."

The man smiled, but his eyes remained grim. "You are quite the negotiator. I'll tell you what I'm looking for. The whereabouts of one of my top men. The FBI took him several years ago. Silvano Estrella. Neither of you are leaving here until I find out where he is."

Savannah moaned then.

"She needs some water," said Cherie.

"I will send in water, then I expect an answer. Or you'll be the next one to feel the effects of my men's wrath. I'm sure they'll have what you *Americanos* call a field day, given the damage you've done to two of their own." Then he turned, the men following him, and left the room.

Seconds later, a guard came in with a bottle of water. After he left, Cherie twisted the lid off and coaxed Savannah. "I've got some water, why don't you take a few sips?"

When her boss raised her head, Cherie bit back a cry. Savannah had blood smeared across her face and one of her eyes was bruised shut.

Savannah's voice came out thick and slow. "How—" She stopped and tried to swallow, grimacing as she did so. "Did you find me?"

"First, take a drink of water."

Savannah took several sips, then several more. "Does anyone know you're here?" she asked Cherie, groggily.

"No. I told Jasmine a few days ago that I'd found something going on here, and she said you were on a hush-hush assignment. Then, the next thing I know, she's MIA."

Savannah shifted in the chair and winced. "That's because she's the mole."

Cherie gasped. Suddenly, she remembered the woman on the beach "That's who's voice I heard. Jasmine's."

"When?"

"It's a long story." She glanced around the room.

"I've already looked for an out." Savannah drank some more water.

"Who does Florencio want to find?"

"His main enforcer and his wife." Savannah cleared her throat. The color was returning to her face. "This was a little before your time. His wife was going to expose Florencio and his operation, in exchange for immunity. We had the Mexican authorities onboard, too."

"What happened?" asked Cherie.

"We think she ran off with the enforcer."

"Think?"

"They disappeared the day we were supposed to secure her official testimony."

"Why not just tell him that his wife ran away with his enforcer?"

"I tried but he doesn't want to hear it." Savannah shook her head slightly. "I wish you hadn't come for me, Cherie. I don't think we're going to get out of this one."

"We will," Cherie assured her. "We'll figure something out."

Savannah gave her a sad smile. "Always the optimist."

While Justin waited for Billy to show up, he checked out the cameras at the compound. When he came to the room where Cherie and her boss were being held, his anxiety went into overdrive. He was relieved to see that Cherie appeared untouched, but her boss looked terrible. Justin wished he had audio on what they were saying. He checked the clock. How were he and Billy going to penetrate Florencio's compound —especially now that his men were on high-alert after Cherie had made her way in?

Justin tapped his fingers on the table. He stared at the computer screen, then got to work hacking into the power grid surrounding the compound. By the time Billy arrived, he'd have the compound's electricity and security at his fingertips.

After she finished the water bottle, Savannah seemed to nod off, mumbling, as if to herself. "I've enjoyed working with you, Cherie. You're a good agent."

"We're going to get out of here." Cherie tried to sound positive, but she knew their odds of surviving weren't good. She thought about Justin then, and her heart felt heavy. He was probably on his way back to the States. How she wished she had told him she loved him when she had the chance.

27

Justin answered the door to find Billy dressed all in black, a duffle bag in hand.

"Thanks for coming," Justin said.

"I should thank you. I was visiting this crazy chick. I don't know what it is about me, but I sure can pick them." He walked into the room and set the bag on the table. "I brought a couple of semi-automatics with night-vision scopes. I'm thinking we need that kind of muscle tonight."

"You got your car back from the hotel?" asked Justin.

"Yeah, and the tank is full."

"We'll have about five minutes after I shut off the power before they turn on the backup generator. Let me show you our route."

When they finished, Billy said, "This Cherie, she means something to you."

Justin ran his hands through his hair. "We need to get her and her boss out alive, or I'll die trying."

"We've been through much worse," Billy assured him. "But you need to get it together before we leave. I've never seen you this unsteady."

Because no one has ever meant this much, thought Justin. This time he had a reason.

"Your time is up, agents," announced Florencio, entering the room, once again flanked by two men. He turned to Cherie. "I trust you've explained to your boss how important this information is to me."

"Yes," said Cherie. "We're going to need access to a computer."

Florencio's eyes narrowed. "You want me to bring you a computer?"

"If you want to know where Estrella is hiding."

"I'll see." Florencio turned on his heel and marched out, the men following.

"You're only buying time," said Savannah in a low voice. "We can't get into Witness Protection's database."

"No, but we can get into the FBI database."

"Then what?"

"Remember that page you had me compile on aliases?"

"For that counterfeiting case?"

The door then burst open and Florencio came in followed by a man, his large stomach hanging over his belt. The man carried a laptop.

"This is my associate Manuel," said Florencio. "He knows computers, so don't bother trying anything."

At that moment, another man skittered in to set up a folding chair and card table. Manuel placed the computer on the table.

"Sit," ordered Florencio.

Cherie sat down and opened the computer while Manuel looked over her shoulder. She quickly typed in her FBI credentials, then navigated her way to the alias database.

Manuel glanced at Florencio. "She is in the FBI database, *Jefe*."

Florencio nodded in approval. "I'm glad to see you are a woman of your word, Agent Tomlinson."

Cherie pointed to the page. "One of these men is the person you're looking for," she said.

"Which one?" asked Manuel.

"I'll let you know once we're out of here."

"You are not leaving this room until you give us the information," said Florencio.

"Then we have a problem," said Cherie. "If I give you the location, there's nothing to stop you from killing us."

Florencio's voice became icy. "I had hoped my men wouldn't have to convince you to comply. Pepe," he said to one of his henchmen, who advanced on Cherie.

"Let's make a deal," said Cherie. "You let Savannah go, and I'll lead your men to Estrella. He's in Mexico. Only an hour from here."

Florencio considered for a moment, his eyes roaming from Cherie to Savannah and back again.

"Agent Sanchez stays here until we have him. Tie her back up," he ordered. Then he gestured to a guard to grab Cherie.

Justin and Billy headed out into the moonless night, ideal for what they had planned. As they approached the compound, a car went flying by in the opposite direction. After the vehicle was out of their rearview mirror, Billy slowed and pulled over to the side of the road. He reached behind the seat. "I've got some Kevlar to put under our shirts. Give us a fighting chance if we get hit."

They got out of the car and helped each other secure the Kevlar with duct tape. Justin put the computer in Cherie's backpack, and they headed toward the compound. When they were several yards away from the back entrance, they stopped in the brush and checked the area. A guard stood outside of the doors talking on his cellphone.

"Pretty quiet out here," whispered Billy.

"That's about to change," said Justin, who had opened the computer and accessed the power grid. "Ready?"

Billy checked the rifles and scopes. "Now we are."

Justin pressed a key. A groaning sound filled the air, followed by complete darkness throughout the compound. He quickly slid the computer into the bag and buried it in some leaves, then took the rifle from Billy.

"On three," said Billy, who took lead. Seconds later, they were flying straight for the guard, now banging on the back-door. Justin hit him close range in the chest and he dropped. Then Billy shot the doorknob off and Justin kicked it in. Inside pandemonium ensued. Justin could see through his scope a guard pulling out a cellphone to light the way. He reached out and grabbed the phone, then twisted the man around into a choke hold. When he passed out and slid to the floor, they continued. At the room Justin was sure held Cherie and Savannah, he pulled the door open while Billy covered him. He saw only Savannah tied to a chair and rushed to her. "I'm here to get you out. Where is Cherie?" He quickly untied her.

"They took her."

"Where?"

"Off the compound."

Justin helped Savannah out of the room while Billy shot rounds into the bodies of two guards. Then they headed toward the door as shots fired behind them. When they were just about out, Justin heard Billy yell. He turned to find he'd fallen to the floor.

"Get him and give me your rifle," said Savannah.

Justin handed Savannah the rifle and reached down to pull Billy to his feet. Then he took ahold of his rifle and draped Billy's arm about his shoulder, helping him along the corridor and out the door. As soon as they were outside, the backup generator kicked on. Savannah fired shots at a guard coming at them.

"The car is a ways up the road," said Justin. "I'm going to need to carry him." He handed the second rifle to Savannah and lifted Billy over his shoulder. "Head east," he said, and they began running. When they got to the trees, he stopped her. "Under the leaves, there's a backpack."

They were close to the car when more shots rang out behind them. Justin pulled the back door open and threw Billy on the seat, then got the keys from his pocket and jumped in to start the car, while Savannah got in the passenger seat. She leaned out the open window as they started driving and fired off more shots.

Once they were out of range, Savannah checked Billy. "He was shot in the abdomen," she said. "We'll have to check beneath the Kevlar for any damage."

Justin drove for several minutes. When he was sure no one was following them, he pulled to the side of the road, got out and yanked the back door open. Savannah helped him remove the duct tape, then they lifted the Kevlar covering his stomach. As they did so, Billy cried out.

"I've seen this before. The bullet pushed some of the

Kevlar into his abdomen," said Savannah. "He has a nasty gash where the Kevlar was, and he'll be badly bruised, but no bullet wound." She picked up an old T-shirt from the backseat and pressed it on the wound.

Relief flooding through him about Billy, Justin asked, "Exactly where did they take Cherie?"

"I need to log on to the FBI database to find Cherie's location," said Savannah.

Justin grabbed the backpack and pulled out Cherie's laptop and handed it to her. Savannah lifted the screen and pressed the power button, but it didn't light up. "I think the battery died. Do you have a charger?"

"Shit, no," said Justin, anxiety making his head throb.

"Give me a cellphone."

Justin gave Savannah his and waited while she dialed a number. He glanced back at Billy, who pressed the shirt to his stomach. His friend caught his eye. "It's just a bad gash like she said."

"Violet, it's me," said Savannah, apprehension in her voice. "I'm okay. But Cherie isn't. I need you to pull up the file of the aliases that she constructed in April. As soon as it comes up, read me the list."

Justin heard a woman's voice on the other end of the line. At one point, Savannah stopped her. "Give me that address again." She ended the call and turned to Justin. "We need to take the 23 north. We're going to 247 Barco, Tesistán."

Justin started the car. "You sure?"

"Positive," said Savannah. "Cherie left a bread crumb. It's the only place on the list that's an hour from here."

"How much of a head start do they have?"

"About twenty minutes."

Cherie sat in the back of the car kicking herself for not having learned better Spanish. At one point, the guards got a call that put them on edge, but all she could make out was something happened at the compound.

"What's going on?" she asked.

The guard in the passenger seat looked back at her, irritation flashing across his face. "*Cállate*," he said. At the confused expression on her face, he translated, "Shut up."

Cherie noticed lights in the distance. Was that their destination? Once they arrived and discovered she was lying, both she and Savannah would be dead.

"Can you pull over? I think I'm about to puke."

The guard glared back at her.

"I'm going to get it all over your nice car." She began to gag.

He turned to the driver and said something, then the man drove to the side of the road. When the car stopped, he ordered Cherie, "*Rapido*, and don't try to run."

Cherie nodded and got out of the car, then went to the back of the vehicle and wracked her brain for some way to get out of this. When her gaze fell on a discarded beer bottle, she grabbed it. Making a loud retching sound, she struck the end of the bottle on the concrete, breaking the bottom off. Then she quickly set the bottle in front of the back tire.

The door to the car opened then, and the guard called out. "Hurry up!"

Cherie stood and walked back to her seat. "Thank you," she said as she slid onto the cool vinyl and shut the door.

Justin drove Billy's car along the highway at top speed. He glanced at Savannah. "What happened at the compound?"

"Cherie is leading Florencio's men on a wild goose chase." Then she looked at him more closely. "She never mentioned you to me. I'm surprised."

Justin glanced at her and back to the road. "We just met."

When the guard started driving again, Cherie heard a crackling sound as the tire ran over the broken beer bottle. She knew it was a long shot, but she crossed her fingers. A few minutes later, the tire blew. Cherie grabbed the sides of the seat as the car bumped across the road. The driver began cussing, his hands gripping the steering wheel as he pulled off the highway.

The two men got out, and she turned to see them inspecting the tire. Then the driver popped the trunk, and the other man began yelling. Did they not have a spare?

As they continued to argue, she noticed that the driver had left his cellphone on the console. When it lit up, she grabbed it and checked the screen. A text that said, *la mujer del FBI ya se fue*. She put the phone back and tried to recall her high school Spanish. They were talking about Savannah, but what did *fue* mean? The men returned to the front of the car then, and the driver checked his phone. He said something to the other guard, who looked back at her and demanded, "Who are you working with?"

"I don't know what you mean."

"Who else knows about the compound?"

"No one," she said.

As the guards proceeded to argue some more, Cherie realized. *Fue* must mean gone. Someone had come to get Savannah. She eyed the dark night beyond the car door. It looked like a cornfield. When the guard started to make a call, Cherie pulled open the door and jumped out, then raced toward the field.

One of the guards yelled after her in Spanish, but she didn't look back. Shots fired as she ran, and she began zig zagging throughout the cornstalks.

Justin slowed the car when he saw a sedan broken down on the side of the road. He braked and pulled up behind it. Both he and Savannah grabbed the rifles, then got out slowly to survey the scene. Three doors were flung open. He went to the driver's side and pulled the latch, then opened the trunk. Empty.

"Looks like they got a flat," said Savannah.

Just then a woman's voice lifted into the night air.

"That's Cherie," said Justin. "It's coming from the cornfield."

29

Cherie had tripped over a rock and was lying on her back when the guard found her. He held a gun on her and growled, "I warned you not to run."

"Savannah escaped, didn't she?" said Cherie. "And you don't have a spare tire."

The guard sneered, "Why don't you worry about your own problems." He reached down and grabbed her by the shirt, pulling her up, then smacked her across the face with his free hand, causing her to cry out. "It'll be much worse if you try this again." He turned them both toward the road, his grip tight on her arm.

Cherie heard the crackle of dry brush and stopped walking a millisecond before the rifle cocked. A familiar voice said, "Put the gun down. Now."

The guard pulled her closer, and said, "I'll shoot her."

Then a rifle cocked from behind them, and another voice said, "This semiautomatic will rip your insides out before you have a chance to think about doing that."

The guard held one arm in the air, then leaned over to put

the gun down as Justin's strong arms pulled Cherie back to him, while Savannah held the guard at gunpoint.

When Justin enveloped her in his embrace, Cherie stood that way for a moment, willing herself to believe this was real. Then she turned to face him. "How?" was all she could manage.

"It doesn't matter right now," he said. "All that does is you're safe."

Savannah cleared her throat and said, "I'm going to take our friend to the car."

"There's another man," said Cherie.

"We've got him restrained," Savannah said.

Cherie pressed her hands against Justin's chest. "I'm so glad you're okay," she said, her breath catching in her throat. "Thank you for finding me."

"I would have found you, no matter what."

"The other night," she struggled to find the words, "in the shower. You said something to me. Did I hear you right, Justin?"

His expression softened. "My words—they're how I feel about you. I can't help it."

"That you love me?" She hesitated. "Anything could have happened to us today. All I could think about was I needed you to know that I love you, Justin. I do."

Justin cradled her face in his hands. "What I didn't add was that I can't see a life without you."

Justin watched as the realization of what he'd just said dawned on Cherie. "What are you saying?" she stammered.

"That you're everything I've ever hoped for. I want your face to be the last thing I see when I turn the light out at night and the first thing I see when I wake each morning."

"Are you asking to marry me?" Her hand went to the base of her throat.

"I know the setting could be better. At heart, I'm a real romantic. But all I want to hear is you say yes."

"Yes, yes, a big yes," she cried, tears glistening in her eyes.

Justin's heart filled at the look of joy on her face.

They went to the Guadalajara police station, where Savannah related the information she had gathered prior to being taken hostage. The police questioned them all separately. Then they took Billy to the nearest hospital to take care of his wound.

Despite numerous tries to get Savannah to see a doctor, she refused. "All I need is a good meal and some sleep," she insisted.

When they were ready to leave, the police captain came clipping into the room, dressed in uniform, and addressed the three of them. "We have completed our investigation and found your stories to be in line. Florencio was arrested thirty minutes ago."

His eyes came to rest on Cherie and Savannah. "I hope you can accept my apology for having been held hostage. Agent Sanchez, we checked the location you indicated and found several American couples being held, as well as evidence of the ransom demands. At first, we were concerned Florencio might slip out of our grasp, but Peter

Baker, the American citizen also being held at the compound, has experienced the operation firsthand and has agreed to testify against Florencio and others in his operation. Our chief is currently speaking with your agency director as to extradition. Florencio will be charged and sentenced in the United States before we sentence him in Mexico. The same goes for Jasmine Garcia."

He smiled then. "I'm sure it has been a most tiring night for all of you. We have arranged for rooms at the Radisson Hotel downtown. And a flight back to the United States tomorrow."

A police car drove them to the hotel and dropped them off, and the three of them straggled to the front desk where Justin explained their circumstances.

Savannah turned to Cherie. "Words will never be enough. Thank you for putting your life on the line to save me. You broke protocol and made some risky moves, but I'm standing here alive, so I'm not going to complain." She glanced at Justin, still speaking to the clerk. "That doesn't mean you don't have some explaining to do when we get back home." She put a hand on Cherie's arm. "I would ask if you're okay, but I can see you're more than fine."

"We're all set," said Justin, handing Savannah her key. "We're on the same floor."

As they headed to the elevator, Savannah said, "I've got to call Brent as soon as I get to my room. He's used to me being out of touch for awhile, but this has been a long one. When does the flight leave tomorrow?"

Justin hit the up arrow. "I haven't had a chance to talk with Cherie yet, but I was hoping she would stay an extra couple of days." He looked at her expectantly. "There's somewhere I want to take her tomorrow."

30

No matter how hard she tried, Cherie couldn't get Justin to reveal anything about their trip the next day. Finally, after they cleaned up and lay in bed in their room, she threw up her arms and slapped them back down on the bed. "Okay, I give up. I guess I'll just have to wait until tomorrow."

Justin laughed, turning to face her. "You'll like it. I promise. It's a really pretty place."

"How do you know I haven't ever been to this pretty place?"

"Because I know you haven't," he said. "C'mon, let's get some sleep. We've got a long drive tomorrow."

"Just tell me something about it. Anything," she pleaded.

Justin smiled. "Okay, fine. It's quiet, and peaceful, and remote."

"Oh, so we can rest and recuperate after all of this," said Cherie, liking the sound of this.

"Exactly." He pulled her to him. "Now, no more questions."

. . .

It was midmorning when Cherie awoke to the smell of coffee. "I can get used to this," she said, raising herself up on one elbow as Justin poured her a cup, stirring in one sugar like she liked it, then handing it to her. "How'd you sleep?" she asked him.

"Better than I have in months." He downed his cup of coffee. "You?"

"Besides waking up a few times curious about today, I slept great. When did you get up?"

"About an hour ago. I made a few calls, including to my father."

"You never told me what happened."

Justin explained how he and his father were questioned about his mother and stepfather. "They've got my stepfather in custody now. I'm still wondering how I missed the signs that my mother was living with a terrorist." He shook his head.

"Terrorists are trained to elude detection," said Cherie. "I've learned that working for the FBI. What's going to happen to your mother?"

"They've been questioning her for two days now, and it looks like she didn't have any idea who my stepfather really was, or what he was engaged in. They're not going to hold her."

"Well, that's a relief," said Cherie. "If you want to go home today so you can see her, I will understand."

"I'll see her soon enough," said Justin. "Drink up. I want to get on the road soon. I already grabbed us some muffins from the breakfast buffet."

When they were settled in the car a few minutes later, Cherie asked, "Which way are we heading?"

Justin adjusted the rearview mirror of Billy's car. Then he started the engine. "You must have been terrible when it came to presents. Did you secretly unwrap them before

Christmas?"

Cherie laughed. "How did you know?"

"Just sit back and eat your muffin. We'll be there before you know it."

Cherie slipped off her sandals and tucked her feet under her. She sighed with contentment. Justin was right. Why not enjoy the intrigue and anticipation?

It was midafternoon when they began descending into a valley. As they drove, the surroundings became greener and the air cooled. "This is beautiful," said Cherie as she gazed out the window.

The deeper they went into the valley, the denser and lusher the terrain became. After a while, Justin slowed the car, then pulled a piece of paper out of his pocket and consulted it. "Keep a lookout up ahead," he said. "There's a drive that is obscured. You'll see a wooden gate."

After they drove a bit more, Cherie pointed. "There."

Justin pulled to the gate and hopped out, consulting the paper as he tapped in a code. He drove through as the gate opened, following along a drive that seemed engulfed by jungle. Cherie looked back to see the gate slide shut. After a couple of minutes, they came to a clearing. There sitting in the sunlight was a little cabin.

"Oh, Justin, this is wonderful! And it's all ours? For how long?"

"Let's go in," he said, undoing his seatbelt.

As they got out of the car, she said, "This is a sweet old place. How did you even know about it?"

It was then that the door opened, and a man stepped out on the porch. At first, Cherie thought they might be trespassing, until she saw the man's face. She pressed a hand to her mouth. "Patrick?" she cried in disbelief, then ran to her brother, who immediately held her to him. "I thought I'd never see you again." She sobbed into his shirt.

Patrick rubbed her back. "It's okay, Sis. Enough water-works. You know I never know what to do when you cry."

Cherie, who thought her heart might burst, laughed then. "But these are the happiest tears I've ever had." She hugged him and lay her head on his chest.

Justin had come up behind them, and she turned to him. "How did you do this?"

"You can thank Billy. I sent him Patrick's photo, and he did the rest."

"But..." began Cherie.

"Still full of questions and protests, I see," said Patrick. He put out his hand to shake Justin's. "Nice to meet you."

Then her big brother opened the door to the cabin. "I know you had a long drive. Come on in and sit down."

At the look of unmasked joy on Cherie's face, Justin knew he'd made the right choice bringing her here. As if she heard his thoughts, she turned to Justin and said, "I can't ever thank you enough." Then she sniffed the air. "Something smells good. Did you take up cooking, Patrick?"

Her brother grinned. "I had to, being on the run all these years. Sit down so we can eat. From what I've heard, you haven't had a decent meal in a while."

Cherie put her hands on her hips. "I see I'm going to have to watch you two talking behind my back."

They sat down at a small wooden table where Patrick

served them *arroz con pollo*. Cherie took a big spoonful and exclaimed, "This is delicious."

When they'd finished eating, Patrick pushed back his chair and glanced from Cherie to Justin. "Now I want to know how you two met."

Cherie set her spoon down. "I would have thought Justin told you."

"Only the broad brushstrokes."

"Then you'll tell me about you?" asked Cherie quietly.

Patrick's expression became serious. "As much as I can."

"Well, Justin actually took me hostage as soon as we met," said Cherie, giggling.

"Funny, Sis," he said. When they looked at one another, he frowned. "You're serious?"

Cherie and Justin proceeded to tell Patrick about the danger and corruption, not leaving anything out. When they'd finished, Justin stood. "I'm going to go outside and leave you two to catch up."

After the door closed behind Justin, Cherie looked at her brother, waiting for him to speak. He picked up the salt-shaker and pushed it around on the table.

"How are Mom and Tad doing?" he asked.

"Mom was promoted at work to head nurse a couple of years ago. And Tad is doing well at college."

"What is he studying?"

"Biology."

Patrick laughed. "I'm not surprised, considering all the strays he brought home. My favorite was the three-legged frog. Boy, did Mom freak out when she found it in the bathtub." He sighed, and his expression became serious. "I'm really sorry for all the pain I caused all of you. There's a lot I can't tell you, but suffice it to say that I was framed, which I think you figured out. By the Genovese family. The only way to keep myself and you all safe was to disappear. And the only way to do that was to make it look like I was dead. Their reach is long and their memory longer. You know that, especially now you're with the FBI, which is really cool, by the way."

"A good part of why I joined the FBI was in the hope of finding you. I wanted to help put things right, and now I can," said Cherie.

"I've said more to you than I should have," said Patrick. "Just know this. I'm working on a plan to get home. It might not be that much longer."

"Patrick." Cherie felt tears starting down her cheeks again. She picked up a napkin and wiped them away. "I imagine you don't want me to say anything to Mom or Tad?"

"Not until I'm closer to a solution." He reached across the table and took her hands in his. "You have to trust me, okay?"

Cherie took a ragged breath. "I've always trusted you. You've been the one person I could always count on. You're my big brother."

After the three of them spent some time talking, Patrick sharing embarrassing stories with Justin about Cherie as a little kid, they said their goodbyes. As Cherie waved at Patrick while they drove away, she said to Justin, "I hate to think of him out here all by himself."

"He's a survivor. He'll be okay."

At the end of the drive when Justin stopped the car to check the road for traffic, Cherie reached over to lay a hand lightly on his leg. "Thank you. You have no idea how much that meant to me."

Justin turned to her.

"I think I do know. I'd do anything for you, Cherie."

"We're a team." She smiled.

"A darn good one," he said, pulling out onto the road. "I was so terrified you would get yourself killed." His voice was full of emotion.

A shiver went through her at his words. "Tell me you love me again," she said, all of a sudden.

"I love you!"

"Louder." She laughed.

He pulled over to the side of the road and took her in his arms for a long kiss. Then once on the highway again, he shouted as they drove back through the thick forest of trees, "I love you. I love you. I love you."

EPILOGUE

Cherie's and Justin's stories are complete, but Patrick Tomlinson's is just beginning....

Patrick Tomlinson got the call just before midnight. He set down the book he'd been reading and answered.

"Yeah?"

"It's time."

"When?"

"The process begins now. You take care of this, it'll all be over."

"I want a guarantee."

The man on the other end of the line took slow, even breaths, then replied, "There will be a sign for you to look for. A yellow rose."

Patrick switched the phone to the other ear. "What?"

"You'll understand when it happens."

He stared up at the roughhewn wooden ceiling of his small cabin. He was so tired of the games, the endless codes, the doublespeak. And of being alone.

"You're telling me a flower is my guarantee for what you

want me to do? Do you know how bat-shit crazy this sounds?"

"Await further instructions. They will arrive shortly."

"That's all I've been doing is waiting—for ten years," Patrick said, his irritation rising. "Hello?" But the caller was gone.

He went to a window and pulled back the curtains to peer out into the dark night of the Puerto Vallarta jungle surrounding his cabin. Was this another one of their head games? Or was this finally his chance to regain his life? He thought about his mother, brother, and sister. Especially Cherie. He'd done everything, including disappear, to protect them.

He sensed movement outside. Grabbing the handgun he kept in the kitchen drawer, he moved quickly to the door, then leaned against it and listened. Above the constant hum of the insects in the jungle, he heard the crackling sound of footsteps on the path. He turned the knob and pulled the door open, ready to shoot, but there was no one standing on the front stoop. Then he heard a car driving away.

Patrick was about to go back inside when he noticed a small, white box at his feet. After picking it up with one hand, he shut the screen and dead bolted the door. Then he took the neatly wrapped parcel to the kitchen and set his gun on the counter. Putting the package to his ear, he listened. Silent. He took out a boxcutter and began to open the missive. Was this the last piece of information he needed?

See what happens with Patrick in *Discovered Escape*.

A NOTE FOR YOU

Dear Reading Gem,

Thanks for spending time with me, Cherie and Justin! While each of the books in the Discovered Truth Series can be read as a standalone, it's fun to experience the progression and get to know the characters. The series progresses as minor characters introduced in each book become main characters in subsequent books. It's exciting to see what they'll do next!

The Discovered Truth series features complex, gutsy women and equally complicated, charismatic men who find themselves immersed in dangerous and intriguing modern-day challenges, such as human trafficking, drug smuggling, organ theft, national security threats, and identity theft. When the heroine and hero meet, worlds collide and sparks fly, kindling unforgettable romance and intrigue.

Thanks again and talk soon!

STAY ENLIGHTENED

Dear Reading Gem, thanks for reading! Let's stay in touch.

Join my weekly newsletter Julie's Reading Gems here. You get a free prequel novella to the series for signing up. There are also weekly giveaways and contests to win free books in the series.

You can also find me on my website at https://www. juliebawdendavis.com/fiction/fiction-books/the-discov ered-truth-series/, email me at Julie@JulieBawdenDavis.com, and follow me on Amazon.

Escape to Unforgettable Romance and Intrigue...

YOUR OPINION MATTERS

If you liked this book, please leave a review on Amazon, GoodReads, BookBub, or all three. If you don't wish to leave a review or don't have time, please leave a rating. Every star helps!

BOOKS IN THE DISCOVERED TRUTH SERIES

Discovered Beginnings:
(FREE at https://www.juliebawdendavis.com/fiction)
Discovered Secrets
Discovered Memories
Discovered Indiscretions
Discovered Liaisons
Discovered Betrayal
Discovered Denial
Discovered Distractions
Discovered Deception
Discovered Lies
Discovered Vengeance
Discovered Redemption
Discovered Obsession
Discovered Transgressions
Discovered Suspicion
Discovered Escape
Discovered Promises
Discovered Cover-up

Box Sets

The Discovered Truth Series Box Set Books 1-4
The Discovered Truth Series Box Set Books 5-8
The Discovered Truth Series Box Set Books 9-12
The Discovered Truth Series Box Set Books 13-16

www.ingramcontent.com/pod-product-compliance
Lightning Source LLC
Chambersburg PA
CBHW022120170626
46808CB00002B/794